I cr...   ...on
the ...

A... ...ull
of b... ...ng
at u...

"...ky
day.

"V... ...le
coul... ...l!"
It w... ...d
then... ...on
the ...

"N... I
wa... ...ff
the... ...l.
"In... ...?,
Tor...

"...

"...

CLUB Sunset Island™

Too Many Boys!

Cherie Bennett

SPLASH™

A BERKLEY / SPLASH BOOK

TOO MANY BOYS! is an original publication of
The Berkley Publishing Group.
This work has never appeared before in book form.

TOO MANY BOYS!

A Berkley Book / published by arrangement with
General Licensing Company, Inc.

PRINTING HISTORY
Berkley edition / June 1994

ISBN: 0-425-14252-3

BERKLEY®
Berkley Books are published by
The Berkley Publishing Group,
200 Madison Avenue, New York, New York 10016.
BERKLEY and the "B" design
are trademarks belonging to Berkley Publishing Corporation.

PRINTED IN THE UNITED STATES OF AMERICA

10 9 8 7 6 5 4 3 2 1

TO JEFF, of course

ONE

"Have you ever been kissed?" I asked my twin sister, Allie, as I contemplated the open magazine in front of me.

She shot me a look of disgust from our closet where she was pawing through her wardrobe, flinging clothes out onto her bed. "No, Becky. I just beamed down from the planet Lovetron where we show affection by drooling on a guy. But only if he's a real babe."

"I wasn't actually *asking* you," I explained. "I was giving you a quiz from *Teen Life* magazine. It's called 'Are You Ready for a Serious Relationship?'"

I scanned the test questions. "Hmm, here's another good one. 'If you're going steady with a guy, do you find it hard to turn down dates with others?'"

"I'm fourteen years old," Allie said, flinging a red miniskirt onto her bed. "I don't want to go steady." She turned to look at me. "You, on the other hand, are practically married, which is totally disgusting." She turned back to the closet. "Do you realize we

1

have nothing to wear to this thing? I'm going to go ask Dad if we can have the credit card to go shopping."

The "thing" she was referring to was our first day as counselors-in-training at the new day camp at the Sunset Island Country Club. Eight of us who were going into the ninth grade in the fall had been picked to be junior C.I.T.s. There would also be six senior C.I.T.s, all going into tenth grade, and ten counselors who were going to be juniors and seniors in high school. The campers would be between the ages of five and twelve.

It wasn't really our idea to become C.I.T.s, to tell you the truth. I mean, every summer we come to our house on Sunset Island—this resort island off the coast of Maine—to have fun, *not* to have responsibility! But Sam—that's short for Samantha Bridges— our au pair, saw this sign up at the club and told our father what a great idea she thought it would be for me and Allie. Dad is under the impression that Sam's a good influence on us—especially because we don't have a mother. That is why at the ancient age of fourteen we have a live-in babysitter. Please don't tell anyone. It's completely mortifying.

I should explain to you about the not-having-a-mother thing. We *do* have a mother. Somewhere. We just don't know where she is. She left our family when me and Allie were just kids. I think maybe she ran off with this younger guy, but Dad won't talk about it so I don't know for sure. Anyway, she left.

Okay, I admit it. I feel funny about that. And about the fact that she never calls or writes. Sometimes I wonder if I did something to make her mad. But then I remember that I was just a little kid, so what could I have done that was really so awful? Usually, I try to tell myself it's my mother's loss, not knowing me and Allie, but sometimes it's hard. You know?

About me and Allie: Sometimes we're the best of friends and sometimes I hate her guts. Of course, if anyone ever said anything bad about her, I would kill them first and ask questions later. We look exactly alike—on the short side of average height, nice brown hair (Allie's is a little shorter), decent figures, decent faces, I guess.

It's weird, though. Some days I look in the mirror and I think I am really cute and other days I am certain I should wear a paper bag over my head because I am such a dog.

The only real way to tell me and Allie apart is that I have a beauty mark over my lip and Allie doesn't. Of course we aren't exactly alike on the inside. Allie is always changing things about herself—like one day she wants to be a nun (and we're Jewish, so that is kind of bizarre), and another day she wants to be a modern dancer. One day she dresses outrageously and wears lots of makeup; the next day she wears baggies and scrubs her face clean. She also loves to read and I hate it. Two of the things we do agree about are Sam and Dad.

About Dad. He's okay. I don't think it's so easy,

being a single father. And sometimes he really messes up. Like he'll be really permissive one minute and totally overprotective the next. That kind of thing drives me crazy. But basically I know he really loves us, and we love him right back.

About Sam. I know I said how excruciating it is that we have a babysitter, but the truth is, we like her. She really is cool. She's nineteen years old, tall and thin, and she has this incredibly great wild red hair. She's been a professional dancer and model. And she's the funniest person I've ever met. I suppose what I really wish is that instead of being my babysitter, Sam was my big sister. Not that I would ever tell *her* that. I figure it would look like a total suck-up.

I have to admit, I'm not always so nice to Sam. It's just that sometimes I feel so angry, like she's only paying attention to me and Allie because my father is *paying* her. I figure if it wasn't for the money, she'd be saying "Becky and Allie *who*?"

And then she'd walk right out on us, just like my mother did.

Anyway, about this C.I.T. thing: Sam told Dad what a good idea it would be for us, and he agreed right away. At first we were totally against it. But then we got to thinking: Wouldn't it be great for a change to tell the kids what to do instead of being the ones who get *told* what to do? Also, Allie and I like little kids. Allie likes all that nature-girl stuff, too, like camping and fishing.

I watched absently as Allie buttoned up a cropped denim shirt and wriggled into a pair of Daisy-Duke cutoff jeans with lace patches. "Hey, do I look fat in these, Becks?"

Pulled from my reverie, I scrutinized her outfit. "It looks okay to me."

"It looks awful," Allie decided, pulling off the jeans. "I mean, that look is so five minutes ago!"

"Gimme a break, Allie. It's camp, not a fashion show," I reminded her, closing the magazine and putting it on the nightstand.

"So?" Allie asked. "I want to make a good first impression." She sat down on her bed and stared at me. "Do you think the other kids will like us?"

I shrugged. "Maybe we won't like them."

"Maybe," she said, scuffing her stocking feet into the rug. "I can't figure out what's right to wear."

"Shorts and a T-shirt?" I suggested.

"Yeah, but what kind?" Allie asked. "Baggy shorts? Tight shorts? Short shorts? And what kind of T-shirt? Plain? With a logo? Tight? Loose?"

"Well, we shouldn't look like we're trying too hard," I mused, which is what I figured Sam would say.

"Okay," Allie agreed. "We have to try really hard to make it look like we're not trying hard, which means we definitely need something new to wear tomorrow. Which means we definitely need the credit card. Hey, Dad!" she called, and hurried out of the room.

5

I threw myself down on my stomach, kicked my legs into the air, and stared out the window. Hopefully, this C.I.T. thing would be fun. The only bad thing about it was that my boyfriend, Ian Templeton, wasn't going to be a C.I.T. with me. I tried to talk him into it, but he wasn't interested.

Actually, he said he would rather eat nails, have toothpicks shoved under his fingernails, and then have his body covered in honey while red ants crawled over him in a feeding frenzy. I took that to mean no.

Ian has much more important things on his mind than being a C.I.T. He may only be thirteen, but he is the head of an incredible, cutting edge rock band called Lord Whitehead and the Zit People. Allie and I sing backup for the Zits. Is that cool, or what?

Ian is very, very serious about his music. That is kind of why I fell for him in the first place. I mean, I had always liked older guys, and for a long time I ignored the fact that Ian had a crush on me. And although Ian is short, wiry, and bites his nails, he is an awesome musician and he's very mature.

Oh, and another thing—believe it or not, Ian is the son of Graham Perry. *The* Graham Perry. He's so famous that he and Billy Joel played a benefit concert together. Well, Ian is just as talented as his father. Maybe even more. It may take a while for the world to understand his music, but it'll happen. . . . And then we will ride off together into the land of the rich and famous, and probably my mother will read about me in *People* magazine, and she'll be really sorry that she ever left us, and she'll call me on the phone and beg me to forgive her.

And then I'll say, "I'll think about it."

TWO

"Do I look okay?" I asked Allie, staring anxiously at my reflection in the mirror.

It was the next morning, and Sam would be driving us over to the country club for Orientation Day at the camp in just ten minutes. Dad had not given us the credit card the day before, which meant we had to make do with what was already in our closet.

"Hey, you were the one who said it was no big thing what we wore," Allie reminded me, sidling up next to me.

I studied our reflections in the mirror, trying to be objective. What would we look like to complete strangers? Allie had on baggy red shorts and a white Minnie Mouse T-shirt Sam had brought from Disney World where she'd been a dancer. I had on khaki shorts and a Yale University T-shirt from one of Sam's best friends, Carrie Alden, who's an au pair for my boyfriend Ian's little sister and who goes to Yale.

Allie had her hair tied back with a red bandanna

and mine was loose. We'd wanted to wear makeup, but Sam talked us out of it. She insists that we are cuter without it. Sometimes I believe her, but sometimes if I'm feeling insecure—which unfortunately is pretty often—I feel better if I put some on.

"We look . . . okay," I decided. "I think."

"Yo, you guys ready to boogie?" Sam yelled from down the hall. Our door was open, and she came by and stuck her head in. "Hey, you two look really cute!" she exclaimed.

"We do not," I mumbled, hoping she would contradict me.

"Listen, you junior fox," Sam said, leaning her arm against the door frame, "I, Samantha Bridges, know cute when I see it. Now, let's get going or you're gonna be late."

The closer we got to the country club, the more nervous I felt. That was really strange, because Allie and I went to the club almost every day to swim and hang out with our friends. But now, going there for a *job,* felt completely different.

"Good luck," Sam called to us cheerfully as we got out of the car. "I'll be back to pick you up at four."

Allie and I were left standing in front of the club. Allie unfolded the letter we'd received from the heads of the camp—a couple named Barbi and Bobby Babbit. It said the staff would meet in the main conference room.

Before heading inside, Allie and I looked at each other, and I could tell she was as nervous as I was.

"If we hate it, we'll give each other a signal," she said. "We'll both pretend to have a terrible stomachache. Then we'll go to the ladies' room and we just won't come back."

I nodded seriously. "That could work." People actually believe that when you're twins you get sick at the same time.

"Okay, pinkie me," Allie said under her breath.

I looked around to make sure no one was looking. Then I quickly brushed my pinkie up against hers. It's our signal from childhood that means we agree on something serious. No one else knows about it. Not even Sam or Dad.

We both took a deep breath and headed for the conference room.

What a zoo. We could hear the crowd way before we actually got into the room. People were running around, laughing, shrieking, and talking at the top of their voices over some really bad rock music that was blaring out of a tape deck with huge speakers. A banner across the front of the room read WELCOME STAFF OF CLUB SUNSET.

"Names?" a girl just inside the front door yelled at us over the music. She looked about sixteen, and was cute, with sun-streaked blond hair and a sprinkle of freckles across her sunburnt nose. She wore cutoff jeans, a Sunset Island T-shirt, and a name tag that read "Liza."

"Allie Jacobs," my sister yelled over the music.

"Becky Jacobs," I added.

"Junior C.I.T.s, right?" Liza asked us.

We nodded.

"Welcome to camp!" she yelled. "I'm Liza Ozur, one of the head counselors." When she said that, I knew she had to be older than she looked, because the camp letter had said the two head counselors were college students.

Liza handed us each a name tag to fill in. "We'll get started soon," she said, "so just go be friendly and introduce yourselves around." She turned to the kids who were standing behind us and we moved into the room.

"Now what?" I asked Allie after we'd stuck our name tags on. The music changed to a rap song, still at a too-loud volume. "Why is that music so loud?" I asked irritably. "How can we meet anyone over that?"

"Hey, are you two twins?" a girl with a thick, long, brown ponytail topped with a baseball cap yelled at us excitedly.

"No, we're a pair of identical strangers," Allie replied loudly. This is one of our stock replies to that annoying question. It may sound really rude, but trust me, we get sick of being asked that.

Fortunately this girl had a sense of humor. She threw back her head and laughed, then she blew a huge bubble with her gum.

"That's really funny!" she exclaimed. "Well, that's what I deserve for asking such a dumb question, huh? My name's Tori Lakeland," she added. She reached into her back pocket and brought out a small Nerf ball, which she threw in the air and caught behind her back.

"Tori's a cute name," Allie offered, working hard to be heard over the blaring music.

"It's a nickname," Tori explained, throwing the Nerf ball again and catching it under one leg. "But I'm not exactly a Victrola, ya know?"

"Your name is really *Victrola*?" I screamed over the music.

"No, I said *Victoria*!" Tori yelled.

Finally someone turned the volume down on the music.

"So, why aren't you a Victoria?" Allie asked in a normal tone of voice.

Tori pulled out two more Nerf balls that had been squished into her back pocket and began to expertly juggle all three in the air. "Oh, you know," she said, casually changing her juggling pattern without missing a beat. "All sweet and refined and girly-girly." She looked around the room. "Like her, for example," Tori said, cocking her head toward a girl in the corner of the room talking with some guy with braces. "Now, *she* looks like a Victoria."

I studied the girl, and Tori was right. Whereas Tori was cute in a fresh, athletic kind of way, the girl in the corner was maybe the blondest, tiniest, most perfect-looking China-doll girl I had ever seen. And whereas Tori had on worn navy blue gym shorts and a red and white baseball shirt, the other girl wore

13

pure white shorts with a knife-like crease in them, a
pristine white T-shirt that looked like no one had
even breathed on, and tiny white ballet flats. Around
her slender wrist was a thin bracelet. Her curly hair
was so blond it was almost white, and it was pulled
back with a slender, white, satin ribbon.

She looked exactly, but *exactly,* how I wished I
looked.

THREE

"Who do you think she is?" Allie asked, studying the girl in the corner.

"I don't know, but I hate her already," I replied.

"How come?" Tori asked, catching all three Nerf balls behind her back.

"She's probably a total snob," I said knowingly. I peered more closely at her. "Is she wearing a diamond tennis bracelet?"

Allie and Tori scrutinized the girl. Her wrist glittered every time she moved it.

"Maybe it's rhinestones," Tori said.

"A girl like that doesn't wear rhinestones," I declared, still staring at the girl.

"Okay, everyone, can I have your attention?" Liza called in a loud voice. "I'm Liza Ozur. I'm one of the head counselors here at Club Sunset, and I want to welcome all of you to orientation."

"And I'm Greg Racer," the other head counselor said, coming up next to Liza. He was impossibly gorgeous, with straight dark hair and huge blue

15

eyes. He had on jeans and a plain blue T-shirt, and he looked nothing short of incredible.

"I'm in love," I whispered to Allie.

"What about Ian?" she whispered back.

All I could do was sigh.

"We've got a lot to do to prepare for the arrival of the kids tomorrow, so we're going to get right into it." Liza continued, "But before we divide into groups, I want to introduce you to the heads of the camp: Barbi and Bobby Babbit!"

The couple ran over to Liza as if they were contestants on "Family Feud," and both of them gave her an enthusiastic high five. Barbi and Bobby looked like they were in their forties, maybe. They were dressed identically in green shorts and green-and-white Club Sunset T-shirts with whistles around their necks. Barbi had her dark hair in a ponytail. Bobby didn't have much hair left, but what was there wound around his head like a swirly soft-serve ice-cream cone. Both of them had huge grins on their faces like they had just won the lottery or something.

"I'm Barbi!" Barbi chirped.

"And I'm Bobby!" Bobby added.

Yeah. Like we couldn't tell who was who.

"We really, really want to welcome you to camp!" Barbi continued.

"Right!" Bobby chimed in. "We think this camp is going to be super. It's especially exciting because we're all starting it together! And Barbi and I want you to know that we're here for you guys. You can always come to us. If you need to rap something out, we'll listen."

"Did he really just say 'rap'?" Allie asked in my ear.

"For sure," Barbi agreed. "And if you want it to turn into a jam session, that's very groovy, too."

Tori rolled her eyes and mouthed *groovy?* at me. I covered my mouth so no one could see me laugh.

"You'll be hearing more from the Babbits later," Liza promised. "Right now, we're going to divide into groups so we can begin to get to know each other. Here's how it works: There are two C.I.T. teams, each consisting of four junior C.I.T.s, three senior C.I.T.s and five counselors. The C.I.T.s answer to the counselors who are the heads of their team, and those counselors answer to either me or Greg."

"And we answer to the Babbits," Greg put in. He consulted the list on his clipboard. "When I call your name, go to either the red team or the blue team side of the room." There was a huge blue happy face on the wall in one corner of the room and a huge red happy face hung catty-corner to it.

"Okay, guys, listen up for the red team," Greg continued. "Liza will be your head counselor." He began to reel off names.

"Tori Lakeland." Tori waved to us, got up, and ambled across the room.

"I hope we're on her team," I said to Allie. "I like her."

"Me too," Allie agreed.

"Allie Jacobs. Becky Jacobs," Greg called.

Bingo. Allie and I walked over to the red happy face. Tori grinned, and the three of us sat down together.

"Ethan Hewitt," Greg called.

Ethan Hewitt! I know Ethan Hewitt! I hadn't even realized he was there, the room was so crowded. Ethan just turned thirteen. Emma Cresswell, Sam's other best friend, is his au pair. Emma is an honest-to-God heiress, which means she's as rich as Princess Di or something.

I waved to Ethan as he walked over to us. I was surprised at how cute he'd gotten and how mature he looked. He was taller than me, with reddish-brown hair and really nice brown eyes. He waved back, looking relieved, and came over to sit with us.

"I didn't even know you'd be here," I told him.

He shrugged. "My parents think this is supposed to build my character or something."

Allie laughed. "Our dad said the same thing. You think maybe they read some kind of secret parent manual or something?"

"So, I heard you and Ian were, like, really tight," Ethan told me.

"Kind of," I admitted.

"They're practically married," Allie snorted with disgust.

"We are not," I insisted. "We're not even going steady." *Now why had I added that?* I wondered.

18

Tori took out her Nerf balls and started juggling while we waited for Greg to finish reading off his list of names.

"You're really good at that," I told Tori.

She shrugged. "It's easy. I can teach you if you want."

"Cool," Ethan said from the other side of me. "I've always wanted to learn to juggle. Could you teach me, too?"

Tori's eyes got big and she blushed. She faltered and dropped a ball.

Then I remembered I hadn't introduced them. "Ethan Hewitt, Tori—I forgot your last name," I apologized.

"Lakeland," she mumbled in a barely audible voice, putting her Nerf balls away. She bit at a fingernail and looked down.

I diagnosed a serious case of guy anxiety.

"Hey, Miss Perfect's name hasn't been called yet," Allie pointed out. I looked across the room and the blond-haired girl was standing there, looking poised and controlled.

"Let's hope she's on the blue team," I said.

"Let's hope she's on the red team," Ethan said, staring with wonder at the girl across the room. "Wow!"

"Oh please, get a life," I snorted.

"And the last person on the red team is Dixie Mason," Greg finished.

It figured. The perfect girl walked confidently

toward us, her posture perfect, her walk perfect, her everything perfect.

Tori smiled at her and moved over so that she could sit with us. I figured that next to this girl I looked like a mutt left out in the rain overnight. If she hung out with us, I would spend the whole summer with the entire world looking at her instead of me.

It would be just my luck.

FOUR

"Okay, red team, let's all sit in a circle," Liza instructed us in a loud voice.

"Hey, sorry, I made a mistake over here," Greg said, running over to us with his clipboard. "You guys ended up with five junior C.I.T.s and blue only has three." He checked his list. "Ethan Hewitt, you should be a blue."

Ethan got up, looking back at Dixie with regret, and went to the other side of the room.

Dutifully we all moved around and formed a big circle. Allie was on one side of me. Dixie-the-Perfect was on the other side with Tori next to her.

"Are you a junior C.I.T.?" Tori asked Dixie.

"Yeh-yus," Dixie replied. "Ah tha-yunk it's go-win tah bey ray-yully gray-yut!" I could not believe my ears. Dixie had a thick Southern accent.

(You get the drift. I don't want to have to keep translating.)

"Yeah, me too," Tori agreed. "Hey, are you Southern?"

21

This was almost as good a line as asking me and Allie if we were twins.

"I'm from Mississippi," Dixie confirmed. "I'm here because—"

"Okay, group!" Liza called. "Let's go around the circle and introduce ourselves. Tell your name, how old you are, and something about you and your family."

"Hey, I took this job to get away from my family!" a cute blond-haired guy joked.

Everyone laughed. It wasn't that funny, but I guess we were all nervous and it broke the tension.

I eyed the kids in the circle as they reeled off information about themselves. The blond-haired guy who had made the joke said his name was Pete Tilly. He was fifteen, going into tenth grade, and his family lived in Portland, Maine.

"I'm involved in Greenpeace and environmental stuff," Pete told the group. "Let's see, what else? My mom is an architect and my dad is a pharmacist. I'm a senior C.I.T. here this summer."

He was darling, really darling, with his straight hair kind of falling over one eye. What was I doing thinking about darling? I couldn't do that; I was in love with Ian. I forced my attention back to the circle.

As everyone told something about his or her life, I noticed that they all mentioned a father *and* mother. This started to get me nervous. Though I read this article in the paper that said that lots of kids are being raised in single-parent homes, evidently none of those kids had been hired to work at Club Sunset.

As more kids spoke and my turn came closer, I got more and more tense. What if having two parents was some kind of criteria for getting hired and they'd just made a mistake on me and Allie? Or even worse, what if they had hired us because they felt *sorry* for us?

"Hi, my name is Tori Lakeland," Tori said cheerfully. "I'm thirteen-and-a-half and I'm going into ninth grade at Sunset High School in the fall. High school—aghhhh!" she screamed.

Everyone laughed, and Tori laughed, too.

"Anyway, I grew up here on the island. My parents own the local health food store, Go Natural, over on Ocean Avenue. Let's see, what else. . . . I have two sisters, a little brother who is a total pain, two dogs, four cats, two rabbits, a hamster, and two horses. Oh yeah, I love sports and I hate health food, especially anything made with tofu."

Everyone laughed again, and I did, too. Tori was so likeable! I saw Pete smile at her, and she blushed and looked away.

"Hey, my name is Dixie Rose Mason," Dixie said in her soft drawl. "I'm not from here—I guess y'all can tell." She laughed at herself. "I live in Starkville, Mississippi, but I'm on Sunset Island for the summer staying with my cousin. I'm thirteen. I have one brother and one sister, and this year my sister is Miss Mississippi—she'll be competing in the Miss

America Pageant this fall in Atlantic City. My parents both teach at Mississippi State University. My dad is a neuropsychologist. I'm interested in baton twirling and science. And I plan to become an astronaut."

I just sat there, totally stunned. This is what I had to follow. Life was totally unfair. I mean, Winona Ryder couldn't have had a cooler resume.

Everyone was looking at me, waiting.

"I'm Becky Jacobs," I began in a froggy voice. I cleared my throat quickly. "And no, I don't even *know* the person sitting next to me," I added, looking over at Allie.

Everyone laughed and I felt a little more confident.

"I'm fourteen," I continued. "I'm in a rock band and I'm really interested in music and, uh, acting. My family has been coming to the island for my whole life. During the year we live on Long Island. In the fall I'll be going into ninth grade at Roosevelt Junior High—" I looked over at Tori. "I only *wish* it was high school."

Everyone was still staring at me like I should say something else, like my life should be more exciting.

"My dad is an accountant," I added lamely.

That was *definitely* not more exciting.

"And my mother is an actress on the soap opera 'Forever Young,'" I added.

Okay. That was a total lie. I have absolutely no idea how that humongous lie popped out of my mouth. Everyone in the circle looked impressed—except Allie, who looked at me as if I had just grown two heads.

Next Allie told about herself, covering the same ground I covered, except that she added she was interested in the environment, and wanted to be a botanist. This got her a smile from cute Pete, and she grinned right back at him.

My head was spinning. I didn't know what a neuropsychologist was, or a botanist for that matter. I had told a whopper of a lie that I couldn't take back. I was stuck with all these people for the entire summer, and I had a dull ordinary life with only one ordinary parent and there was no way out.

I frantically gave my sister the signal that meant we should both get stomachaches and run to the ladies' room, but she was too busy making eyes at Pete to notice.

"Okay, I'm passing out the basic camp itinerary," Liza said when the introductions were finished. "I'd like you to form smaller groups now, counselors with counselors, senior C.I.T.s with senior C.I.T.s, et cetera. Talk about what you're good at so we can divide up camp activities. Just write your name by the activities you excel at. I'll come around to each group." Then she passed out a bunch of sheets of paper stapled together.

"Junior C.I.T.s is us I guess," Tori said, and she and Dixie swung around to face me and Allie.

"So, who's good at what?" Tori asked, scanning a list on the first sheet of paper. "Archery?"

"Yeah, like I've got a bow and arrow in my purse," I replied.

Tori laughed heartily. I love anyone I can make laugh.

"No one, huh? Okay, how about badminton?"

"We can do that," Allie said, speaking for me, too. "I mean, we don't *excel* at it, but we could teach a little kid, I guess."

"Good," Tori said. She looked back at the list. "Baton-twirling—I guess that's you!" she looked over at Dixie.

"Sure!" Dixie agreed happily.

We continued down the list. Allie signed up for campfires and nature walks, I signed up for drama and creative writing, and we both signed up for music. In addition to baton twirling, Dixie took cheerleading, camp spirit (whatever that was), crafts, and dance. Tori had by far the longest list, including every sport known to mankind.

"This list is kind of lopsided," Liza said when she got over to our group.

"I don't mind teaching other people some of this stuff—that is, if you guys want to learn, Tori said."

"Well, we'll work it out," Liza replied. "Now, you guys are going to be mainly responsible for the littlest kids, the five to seven year olds. We're expecting thirty of them, which means fifteen will be part of the red team. On page two you'll find the schedule for tomorrow." She continued, "Whenever you guys have any kind of a problem, you check with Pete, okay?" she said.

Allie looked very happy to hear that she had to check in with Pete on a regular basis. I figured she'd be making up reasons to check in with him as often as possible. Well, that was okay. It didn't matter to me. I had a boyfriend.

"Okay, well, why don't you guys take a little longer to get to know each other," Liza suggested. "Then we'll take a tour of the facilities and the camp grounds." She walked over to the senior C.I.T.s.

"Gee, I can't believe we have to report to Pete," Allie said in a deadpan. "What a drag."

Dixie smiled. "Meanin' you think he's cute."

"Don't you?" Allie asked her.

Dixie looked over at Pete. "I guess he is," she agreed, "but this is as close as I'll probably ever get to him, so it doesn't make much difference."

"But you're gorgeous!" Tori blurted out, in what I was beginning to realize was typical Tori fashion. "You could get any guy on the entire planet!"

Dixie smiled. "That is so sweet of you," she said, and she really seemed like she was being sincere and not simpy. Believe me I would have preferred to hate for her being self-confident, but now I couldn't.

"What I meant was—" she continued seriously, her eyes searching our faces. "Promise you won't tell?"

"Sure," I said, since I had absolutely no idea what she was talking about. Allie and Tori agreed, too.

"Well, the thing is," Dixie explained, "my parents won't even let me near a boy. Ever."

FIVE

Allie's jaw hung open. "Ever? I mean, *ever,* ever?"

"Pretty much," Dixie admitted with a sigh. "My father says I can't date until I'm eighteen."

Now it was my turn to hang my jaw open. "Eighteen?" I repeated. "What planet is your dad living on?"

"Sometimes I ask myself the same question," Dixie said sadly. She moved closer to us confidentially and clasped her knees with her arms. "But I went on a hayride, and this boy I knew from church actually held my hand!"

I cocked my head to one side. "Wait a second. Are you for real?"

She shook her head seriously. "My parents are just ridiculously strict," she explained. "I guess y'all have had tons of boyfriends, huh?" she asked me and Allie.

"Well, sure," I replied. "My boyfriend right now has his own rock band."

"And I'm hanging out with, like, three or four

different guys," Allie added. "I mean, I'm not serious with any of them. I'm just having fun."

"Fun," Dixie echoed with longing. "I'd like to have fun." Then her eyes lit up. "Which is why I wanted to come here this summer so badly!"

"Because your parents are far away, huh?" Tori asked.

Dixie nodded. "I just want some freedom for a change! So I begged to come and visit my cousin, Molly. She swore on a stack of Bibles she'd watch over me, which is the only reason my parents agreed to cut me loose," Dixie rushed on. "Of course, Molly is wild—her friends call her Maniac Mason"—Dixie giggled—"but my parents don't know that. She lives here on the island with my aunt and uncle in this big ol' spooky house, and—"

"Wait a second," I interrupted. "Do you mean Molly Mason? I know Molly Mason!"

"She's been over at our house lots of times," Allie put in eagerly. "She's really good friends with . . . this older friend who lives with us," Allie said, careful not to refer to Sam as our au pair.

"Isn't Molly the greatest?" Dixie exclaimed. "I love her to death."

"So, I guess you know Darcy Laken, too—Molly's friend who lives with her and helps take care of her since her car accident."

"She's cool, too!" Dixie exclaimed. "The two of them have all these adventures together! No one has adventures at my house.

"My parents always know what I'm doing, every single second of the day," Dixie said with a sigh.

Tori snorted. "Not mine. In fact, my parents are so busy they never know *what* I'm doing. My house is kind of a zoo—there are more animals than people, anyway."

Dixie turned to look at me with her huge, cornflower blue eyes. "Your mom is really a famous actress on 'Forever Young'?" she asked me.

Allie nudged me hard in the ribs. She seemed to be reminding me that this was my chance to say it had all been a big joke.

I ignored her.

"Yeah, she sure is," I replied.

"I watched that soap when I was home with the flu," Dixie said, clearly impressed. "What character does she play?"

Oops. "Uh . . . she does . . . guest appearances," I improvised. "She's too big of a stage star to work on that show all the time."

"Wow," Dixie breathed. "What's your mom's name?"

"Talia," I said. "Talia . . . French!"

I had absolutely no idea where that name came from.

Dixie's eyes got even bigger. "Dang, I think I've heard of her!" she exclaimed.

"Not me," Tori said. "But don't feel badly. We don't own a television."

Now we all turned to Tori.

"You don't own a TV?" Allie marveled.

"Nope," Tori said matter-of-factly. She took out her Nerf balls and began to juggle. "My parents think that television is one of the great evils of the century." She popped a Nerf ball off her elbow and brought it smoothly back into her juggling pattern.

"You don't watch MTV?" I asked in shock.

"Sure, when I go to my friends' houses," Tori explained.

"Hi, how are you guys doing?" Pete asked, coming over to our group. He knelt down and dropped his hand lightly on Tori's shoulder. She froze.

"We're doin' great," Dixie replied easily, grinning at Pete.

"Cool," Pete said. "So, have any of you gone to camp before?"

"Cheerleading camp," Dixie said. She raised her eyebrows. "All girls, of course," she added emphatically.

"Not us," Allie told him. "So you may need to give us extra help."

Yeah, right.

"Sure thing," Pete agreed. His arm was still on Tori's shoulder. "How about you?"

"I . . . uh . . . I . . ." Tori stammered.

"Oh yeah, she's been to tons of camps," Dixie explained, covering for Tori. "She told us all about it. She's great at camp!"

Pete gave Tori a funny look. "Well, okay. So, I'll see you guys later."

As soon as he walked away Tori dropped her head into her hands. "I hate myself! I am a slug! I am a sub-slug!"

"No—" Dixie protested.

Tori lifted her head. "Did you see the way I just acted around him? I couldn't talk. I couldn't move. I couldn't even breathe! I'm amazed that I'm still alive!"

"You're just shy," Dixie said in a kind voice. "It's okay to be shy."

"Sure, lots of girls are shy," I agreed so that Tori would feel better. Actually, she had the worst case of guy-shyness I had ever personally witnessed, but I certainly didn't want to tell her that.

"I will never have a boyfriend," Tori wailed.

"Sure, you will," Dixie insisted.

"I bet you meet so many boys this summer that you end up with tons of boyfriends," I added supportively.

"If I don't keel over from lack of oxygen just because a guy looks in my direction," she moaned.

"Now, don't you worry," Dixie told her. "We'll help you." She turned to me. "Not that I have any actual experience in that department, myself," she added with chagrin. "Y'all are so cool," she said. "I mean, your mom is famous, and you've had lots of boyfriends and all. I was thinking maybe . . . maybe you could kind of give me and Tori boy lessons."

Dixie and Tori stared at me and Allie hopefully.

33

Allie and I looked at each other and grinned and secretly pinkied each other behind our backs.

"Girls," I said confidently, "you are in for the summer of your lives."

SIX

"Hey, this kid just hurled! Gross! Total gross-out!" a little boy shouted, pointing at a kid who was bent over heaving into the grass.

"Hey, I have to go to the bathroom!" a skinny girl in a red T-shirt and oversized jeans yelled, her hands on her hips. "How am I supposed to go to the bathroom when you've got us out in a *field*?"

"I'll go after the barfer. You go after the prima donna," Tori suggested to me, and we took off in opposite directions.

It was the next morning, and the field next to the country club was swarming with kids. Each one had been given a red or blue circle to pin on his or her shirt. The C.I.T.s were supposed to gather the kids for their team and lead them over to the leader—in our case, Liza.

"Hi, I'm Becky," I told the girl who wanted to use the bathroom. "I'm a C.I.T. here."

"What's that stand for? Completely Irritating and Tacky?" she grumbled. Her smart mouth didn't match her looks at all. She was tiny and pale, with a long blond braid sticking out of the back of a red baseball cap. She looked about eight years old.

"It stands for counselor in training," I explained patiently, since I figured I could probably get fired if I smart-mouthed a little kid on the first day of camp. "You're on the red team, right?"

She looked down at her shirt where a red circle was pinned. "If that's what this dumb circle means," she replied. Her voice was low and scratchy. She sure didn't *sound* like an eight year old. She crossed her legs tightly. "Listen. I really, truly gotta go. And I'm not squatting in this field."

"Well, I guess it's okay if you go inside," I told her. "There's a girls' room in the hallway to the right, just off the lobby."

"Cool," she replied. "Oh, by the way, have you got a butt?"

"Uh, yeah," I said. "Last I heard everyone had one."

"I mean a cigarette butt," the girl explained, rolling her eyes at my stupidity.

"You *smoke*?" I asked her incredulously.

"No, I chew them up and spit the tobacco at cute guys," she replied sarcastically.

She reminded me of someone; I couldn't think of who. I cocked my head to one side. "Just how old are you, anyway?"

"Thirteen," she said with bravado.

"You can't be. Campers only go up to twelve," I

pointed out. "Besides, you definitely don't look thirteen."

"Says you," the kid shot back. "Well, I'm outta here. Catch you later." She took off for the clubhouse.

"Weird, really weird," I muttered. I looked around. Allie was filling in names on a bunch of kids' red circles. Dixie was helping Tori with the kid who had been throwing up. I walked over to another bus that had just arrived.

"Hi, welcome to Club Sunset!" the counselors were calling to the kids as they got off the bus.

"Blue team to the right, red team to the left!" Greg called out over and over.

"It's okay, Kira," a little African-American girl was saying to another girl who was crying near the bus. "We'll see each other all the time."

"But I want to go where you go!" the girl sobbed.

I walked over to them. "Can I help? I'm Becky."

"I'm Shyla Medgar, and this is my best friend, Kira Mironov," the black girl said in a clear voice. "She just moved here from Russia a few weeks ago. We live next door to each other. She doesn't know anyone but me, but they put her on the red team and me on the blue team."

"Please, I want to be with Shyla," Kira said with a thick accent, taking her friend's hand.

"Did you ask that guy over there if you could switch?" I asked them, pointing to Greg.

"We did ask," Shyla replied. "He said he'd have to check because it might mess up his lists."

Both girls stood there holding hands, staring up at me like I could fix everything.

Just then a boy walked by with a blue circle on his T-shirt. He was walking with another kid who wore a red circle. I had an idea. "Hey, are you two guys friends?" I asked them.

"Yeah," one kid said. "We're on the same Little League team."

"I bet you'd like to be on the same team here, too, huh?" I asked him.

He shrugged. "Yeah, that'd be okay."

"Great," I said, and quickly unpinned his red circle and traded it for Shyla's blue one. "You just got your wish." The two boys ran off, and I pinned Shyla with the red circle. "There, now you two are on the same team."

"Thank you!" Kira cried, hugging me hard. "You are most wonderful!"

Shyla took my hand. "Are we on your team?" she asked me hopefully.

"You got it," I confirmed. "Now, you guys go over there with the red group. I'll be there soon."

They scampered off and I felt like a million dollars. I made a mental note to tell Greg about the change. I hoped he wouldn't mind too much.

"I am so grossed out," Tori said, coming up next to me. "That kid has been barfing for the past fifteen minutes."

"Where is he now?" I asked her, since I didn't see him in the field anymore.

"Dixie took him inside to the nurse," she explained, brushing a strand of hair off her face. "I hope I didn't get any of that stuff on me. Do I stink?"

I sniffed her. "No, you're okay."

"Excuse me, I'm Muffy Sue Courtland," a sweet, Southern voice tinkled. Her accent was different from Dixie's, not quite as thick. I looked down, and there was this kid, about seven was my guess, wearing a pink ruffled jumpsuit, white tights, and party shoes. Her long, dark curls were held back by a huge pink bow. I couldn't be sure, but I thought she was wearing mascara and blush. "Can you tell me where I'm supposed to go, please?"

Tori and I exchanged looks.

"Which team are you on, Muffy?" I asked.

"It's Muffy Sue," she corrected me. "I don't know which team I'm on. I didn't get one of those little circles."

"I am praying that little boy doesn't have the stomach flu," Dixie said, coming over to us. "Because if he does we'll all get it, and then—"

"Dixie Rose!" Muffy Sue exclaimed in awe. "Dixie Rose Mason?"

Dixie looked over at Muffy. "Yes?"

"You *are* Dixie Rose Mason!" Muffy Sue squealed. "Oh, I am just so proud to meet you!"

"What is it, everyone with a Southern accent

knows everyone else with a Southern accent?" I asked.

"Don't you know who she is?" Muffy Sue asked me. "She is just the most famous Little Miss Sweetheart of all the Little Miss Sweethearts!"

Tori made a face. "I think I'm missing something here," she said.

"Listen, sweetie, we don't really need to talk about that—" Dixie began, putting her hand lightly on Muffy Sue's arm.

Muffy Sue grabbed it reverentially. "Oh, let me tell it." Muffy Sue closed her eyes and recited. "Six years ago in Atlanta, Dixie Rose Mason from Mississippi was crowned America's Little Miss Sweetheart. She was the most talented, smartest, most beautiful Little Miss Sweetheart ever. Dixie Rose visited poor children and children in hospitals. Once she visited a little girl in a coma, and right after that the little girl woke up and started speaking! And Dixie Rose could tap dance better than the Rockettes at Radio City Music Hall in New York City."

"Oh well," Dixie said, her face burning with embarrassment, "that was a long time ago and—"

"I grew up hearing about Dixie Rose," Muffy Sue went on. "We used to play with dolls we named Dixie Rose! I tried for three years to win the pageant, just so I could be like Dixie Rose!"

"It's just Dixie, really—"

"And this year I did it!" Muffy Sue squealed. She pulled a tiny tiara out of her back pocket and perched it on her head. "I am America's Little Miss Sweetheart!" She leaned in to us confidentially. "I just think it's tacky to show off and wear my crown all the time, don't you?"

"Oh yeah, I usually leave my crown home, too," Tori agreed, trying to keep a straight face.

"Imagine," Muffy Sue said with wonder. "I came all the way here to visit with my big cousin Lorell, and I run into Dixie Rose Mason. I just have to be on your team, Dixie Rose!"

"You know, that is such a shame," Dixie said. "I remember seeing your name on the list for the blue team."

"Oh no!" Muffy Sue wailed.

"So you just run on over to the blue team," Dixie told her sweetly. "But I'm sure we'll see you often." Dixie waved as Muffy Sue wandered forlornly over to the blue team. "Bye-bye, now!"

"Was she really on the blue team?" Tori asked Dixie.

"She is now," Dixie replied. "And please forget everything you heard her say about me."

"America's Little Miss Sweetheart?" I asked Dixie.

"My mother used to put me in all these beauty pageants when I was a little girl," Dixie explained, rolling her eyes. "I quit them when I was ten—I just simply refused to do it anymore. My mother took to her bed and cried for three days. Fortunately for my mother, my big sister, Crystal, has kept on for her

41

whole life. It's my mother's dream to have one of her daughters crowned Miss America."

"Scary," Tori commented.

"Please don't tell anyone," Dixie begged us.

"Oh, we won't," I promised. "I think it's the current Little Miss Sweetheart you have to worry about."

Liza blew her whistle and began to speak into a microphone. "Could everyone please sit down now so we can get started?"

Tori, Dixie, and I hurried over to the red team. I looked around for Allie. She was talking with Pete Tilly, but quickly came over to join us.

"Tell me he isn't the cutest," she said to me.

"Ian's cuter," I said back.

"Yeah, in your dreams," she snorted.

"Who's Ian?" the girl with the froggy voice asked, ambling over to me.

"My boyfriend," I told her. "What's your name, by the way?"

"Jodie," she replied.

I introduced her to Allie, Tori, and Dixie.

"You're all C.I.T.s?" Jodie asked. "What, am I supposed to, like, listen to you four or something?"

"That's who you remind me of!" I exclaimed, snapping my fingers. "Jodie Foster when she was a little kid! I saw her in these old movies we rented! You look like her and you sound like her!"

"Yeah, that's right," Allie agreed.

"I wouldn't know," Tori put in with a sigh. "I only

get to see movies that don't promote decadent values—whatever that means."

"Well, we'll rent the grossest movies we can find one night," I promised Tori.

"Thanks," she said gratefully.

I turned back to Jodie. "It's really an amazing resemblance."

"Yeah, well, everyone tells me I sound like Jodie Foster when she was a kid, and I look like Jodie Foster when she was a kid. Big, bad deal," the girl said.

"How old are you, really?" I asked her.

"Thirteen," she admitted. "And don't tell me how small I am for my age, okay?" She plopped down next to me on the grass.

"Welcome to Club Sunset Island!" Liza called into the microphone. "I'm Liza, this is Greg, and we're really happy to have all you campers here!"

Barbi took the microphone from Liza. "I'm Barbi Babbit," she said.

"And I'm Bobby Babbit," her husband said, leaning into the microphone. He turned and motioned Greg and Liza over. "We prepared a little cheer to kind of welcome you to Club Sunset," he continued. "Okay, you guys ready?"

> Four, three, two, one,
> Club Sunset's so much fun!
> One, two, three, four,
> Stick around we'll tell you more!

> Ten, nine, eight, seven,
> Our camp is just like heaven!
> Seven, eight, nine, ten,
> Let's do our cheer again!

"Come on, kids, join in!" Barbi called gaily. "Let's get the spirit!"

"I hope she doesn't quit her day job," Jodie muttered to me. I stifled a laugh.

The counselors all started to chant again, and the kids began to join in. We joined in, too, although I have to say I felt like an idiot.

At the end of the cheer everyone yelled "hoorah," and Barbi and Bobby jumped up and down, clapping their hands. The little kids seemed to love it, while some of the older kids made gagging gestures. Not that I could blame them. Greg sang out.

> All for the blue team,
> Stand up and holler.
> And if you can't hear us,
> We'll yell a little louder!

Lisa Yelled back.

> All for the red team,
> Stand up and holler.
> And if you can't hear us,
> We'll yell a little louder!

Soon everyone on both teams was screaming for their team. I couldn't help it; I got into it in spite of myself. If someone had told me that I, Becky Jacobs, would be standing in a field screaming about team colors with a bunch of little kids, I would have told them they were crazy.

But to tell you the truth, it was fun. Tori did a mean whistle at the end with two fingers in her mouth. Everyone seemed to be having fun, except Jodie, who just stood there with her hands shoved into the pockets of her jeans.

After our cheering session, Barbi rattled off which age group of kids went to which activity at what time. Then she talked about some of the special camp activities coming up. "Later on in the summer, we'll have a color war with Camp Eagle. They're across the bay on Eagle Island.

"But let's talk about some of the really far-out stuff that's coming up sooner than that," Barbi continued. "Let's see, there's camp skit day, and the white-water rafting trip, and the spook-out overnight, and well, just tons of things!" she gushed.

"Right on, Barbi!" Bobby agreed with enthusiasm.

"This guy is in a serious time warp," Jodie said. "Hello, this isn't the sixties!"

"And don't forget," Barbi added. "Next Tuesday— one week from today—we'll have our Welcome to Club Sunset Parents' Day. We have one at the beginning of camp and another one at the end. That way your parents can see just what camp is like and

45

also see all the cool things you've accomplished by the end of the summer!"

"Oh great!" Dixie exclaimed, turning to me. "That means we'll get to meet your mother!"

"Who's her mother?" Jodie asked.

"Just the famous actress Talia French!" Dixie told her.

"Gee, she might be busy shooting her soap opera in New York," Allie said, shooting me a nasty look.

"Oh, she has to come!" Dixie cried. "You'll call and ask her, won't you? Please?"

Believe it or not, I said yes.

SEVEN

"Of all the dumb things you've done in your life, this is the dumbest," Allie said to me on the way home late that afternoon. Of course she was referring to the Talia French situation.

The first day of camp had otherwise been okay. I supervised the youngest kids during free swim, and I got to lead a sing-a-long with Allie. But word had spread through the entire camp about our famous mother, and Barbi Babbit herself came up to me and Allie to tell us how "far-out" it was that our mom was going to come to their camp for Parents' Day. Then she assigned us to help out with the Club Sunset Follies, which she explained was a show of music and skits put on for the entire camp.

One thing was for sure, this camp thing was seriously hard work, and by the time the kids were getting on their buses to go home at four o'clock, I was pooped. The last thing Bobby Babbit said to me when Sam came to pick us up in my dad's car was, "Maybe you could ask your mom to bring some

47

autographed pictures when she comes for Parents' Day."

"Sure thing," I had replied, while my sister glowered at me. As soon as Sam pulled out of the country club parking lot, Allie really let loose on me.

"I mean, you are nuts. Truly nuts!" Allie shrieked.

"Thanks, I love you, too," I replied in a sour voice, turning up the radio to drown her out.

Sam stopped the car at a light and gave me a look, then asked Allie, "What did she do?"

"We don't want to talk about it," I said quickly.

"Right," Allie agreed, "because it makes *one* of us look like a total butthead."

Sam turned down the volume on the radio. "So, how did you like the first day with the campers?"

"It was okay," I said. I wasn't in the mood to chat. I had to think up a plan. Maybe I could say my mother was in a Broadway show and she couldn't possibly get away to come to some stupid camp thing. But what if someone asked me *what* Broadway show? Or what if someone actually checked?

I was in deep doo-doo.

As soon as we got home, Allie and I went straight up to our room and threw ourselves on our beds, exhausted.

"What am I going to do?" I wailed.

"I don't know, kill her off or something," Allie suggested. "Have her get into a car accident."

"That's gruesome," I shuddered.

"Okay, say she's in Europe," Allie improvised.

"She's . . . she's the model for a new perfume, and she's on a promotional trip around the world getting her photo taken and her wrist sniffed."

"Stupid idea," I said, and turned over on to my stomach. "We've got a major problem."

"*You've* got the problem," Allie corrected me.

"She's *our* mother, so it's *our* problem," I pointed out.

And then a truly terrible thought came to me. Even if I could figure out a lie good enough to fool everyone at camp, there was no guarantee that people wouldn't ask Dad about his wife, the famous actress. In fact, I was sure they would ask.

And I couldn't very well tell him I had made her up. I quickly related this little wrinkle to Allie.

"We're totally ruined," Allie said with finality. "We can never show our faces at that camp again. And it's your fault."

"Hey, how are my girls?" Dad asked, appearing at just that moment in the doorway.

"Great," I said offhandedly, like I didn't have a concern in the world.

"Was camp fun?"

"Sure," Allie said flatly. "The funnest."

"I knew you guys would like it, once you gave it a chance," Dad said, beaming at us. He came into the room and sat down on Allie's bed. "I need to talk to you about something. Sam!" he called.

She came to the doorway. "You rang?" she asked.

"I thought we'd talk to the girls now—"

"The two of you are running away together?" Allie guessed.

Sam made a face.

"Not amusing," Dad replied.

"I don't know why," I said. "The women you date aren't that much older than her."

"Who I date is my private affair," Dad said evenly.

"How come who I date isn't my private affair, then?" Allie asked.

"Because I am the parent, and you are the kid," Dad said.

"Figures," Allie mumbled.

Dad reached over and pulled her hair playfully. "Actually, I wanted to talk with you girls about some travel plans of mine," he said. "There's an accountant's convention in Boston next week, and I'd like to go."

I sat up on my bed. "When next week?" I asked quickly.

"Tuesday through Thursday," he explained. "I'm going to leave Sam in charge."

"Dad, please," Allie snorted, "we can be in charge of ourselves. That is so humiliating!"

"No, it's great!" I said jumping up. "Yes, siree, kids need structure. That's what I always say!"

Everyone in the room looked at me like I had lost my mind.

"And Sam is really mature and everything," I rushed on, "and we'll listen to everything she says, won't we, Allie?"

50

"Have you been sitting too close to the microwave?" Allie asked with amazement. "Your brain cells are rattled."

"Ha!" I barked. "Funny! Gee, Allie, too bad Dad won't be here *Tuesday*." I emphasized Tuesday so she'd catch my drift—no Dad on the island meant no Dad at Parents' Day! Which meant no one could ask Dad about his wife, Talia French!

"Oh yeah," Allie agreed, finally catching on. "Have a great time, Dad."

"And thanks for this great little chat," I added cheerfully. "Don't you worry about us any!"

"That's my girl," Dad said. He came over to my bed and kissed me on the forehead. "Well, I'm glad we worked this out. See you later!" He ambled out of the room.

Sam put her hands on her hips and gave me a jaded look. "Okay, what's up?"

"I have no idea what you're talking about," I replied innocently.

"'Kids need structure'?" Sam repeated.

"Well, adults always say that," I explained. "And adults love it if you repeat back to them the stuff they say."

"Yeah, I realize that," Sam replied. "What I'm asking is, what are you up to that you shouldn't be up to?"

"It's private and personal," I said with dignity.

"Well, cool," Sam said, "as long as it's legal."

I looked over at Allie. "She has no faith in us."

"Personally I am deeply insulted," Allie agreed.

Sam threw her hands up in the air. "I give up!" she cried, and turned and left the room.

I ran to the doorway and looked around. "Okay, the coast is clear," I reported, plopping back down on my bed.

"Yeah, now we have no parents coming to Parents' Day," she pointed out.

"Wrong," I said. "I have a plan. An incredible, foolproof plan. What we need is someone who can pretend to be our mother for the day."

"You're kidding," Allie said flatly.

"I'm totally serious," I insisted. "How tough can it be? I mean, no one has really seen Talia French because she doesn't exist, so all we have to do is find someone who can pull it off!"

"Who?" Allie asked. "Sam?"

"Too young," I figured. "Besides, too many of the people at camp know who she is. Now, who do you hire if you need someone to pretend to be an actress?"

"I give up," Allie said. "Who?"

I grinned. "Simple! You hire an actress!"

"I'm telling you, this is going to be perfect," Ian insisted, as he, Allie, and I floated on rafts in his pool later that night.

I had called Ian and let him in on my dilemma. I kind of had to. I mean, I didn't know any actresses. And I certainly couldn't call up some agency and have a bunch of actresses come parading around my house to audition.

Ian, on the other hand, knew lots of people in show business because of his father. He also had something I didn't have: his own back account. Whoever we hired was going to have to be paid.

Ian thought the whole situation was very dramatic—he loves drama, and in fact said he'd probably write a song about this for the Zits—and he invited me and Allie over to plan everything. Dad had a date with someone named Julie, so Sam had dropped us off at Ian's. Fortunately, everyone else at the house was inside.

At first Ian narrowed down the choices to an actress in Bangor who had been in one of Graham's music videos, and a singer on Eagle Island who used to sing with a group that had opened for Graham's band.

He went inside and looked up the number of the woman in the video in his dad's phone file, and then called her house. He explained who he was, emphasizing the "Graham Perry's son" part. He kind of implied that he was calling for his father. Then he explained that he had an acting job that would only involve a couple hours of her time and that she was invited to hang out at Graham's house afterward.

She said yes before he could finish.

Now we were hanging out at the pool, waiting for this actress to show up.

"What's her name again?" I asked Ian nervously.

"Kiki Coors," Ian replied. "You'll like her. She's really pretty."

"He-lloooo!" a female voice finally trilled. "Anybody home?"

"Back here!" Ian called, trying hard to make his voice sound deep, like his dad's.

"Graham, your house is just so huge and fabulous!" Kiki cried. She kept up some bright patter as she came closer to us, and then stopped when she looked down at three kids floating in a swimming pool. She didn't look terribly thrilled, I gotta tell you.

Well, I wasn't so terribly thrilled myself.

Kiki teetered on ridiculously high platform sandals. She wore skintight leopard-print Lycra pants and an orange frilly blouse that barely covered her oversized bosom. Her bleached blond hair was piled up on her head, and orange lipstick was smeared across her lips.

I knew what Sam would say: Get the fashion police!

All bets were off. I would rather be an orphan. No way was I passing this woman off as my mother.

EIGHT

Let me make one thing clear: I am ordinarily not a big, fat liar. Once I heard someone describe it like this: When you tell a lie, it's like dumping a pillowcase full of feathers off a high cliff. You can race down to the bottom and try to gather up all those feathers, but no matter what you do, there's no way you can collect each and every feather.

In other words, the lie spreads itself around, and you just get in deeper and deeper and deeper.

Well, the next day at camp it seemed to me as if everyone was talking about my famous mother who was going to be visiting the camp on Parents' Day. Ethan even came over to me to ask about it, saying he'd never heard that my mom was a famous actress—in fact, he thought he'd heard Emma and Sam saying that my mom ran out on us when me and Allie were little kids.

Of course I told him he was completely mistaken.

Shyla asked if she could write a poem for my mother, that she and Kira would act out. Muffy Sue planned to bring in her picture and resume, so that "Mom" could help her get a role on "Forever Young."

I was a desperate girl. Which is why I decided to call Ian during lunch, and tell him to call Kiki, and tell her she had gotten the gig after all. Like I said, I was desperate.

The night before, we had told Kiki that we were auditioning several actresses and that we'd call her. Of course, we never planned on calling her. She kept asking why three kids were interviewing for Graham Perry and Ian kept dodging the question. She was pretty ticked off when she left Ian's house.

But now I had a plan. I had instructed Ian to tell Kiki to be at my house at seven that evening. Dad had another date with this Julie person, and Sam had a date with her boyfriend, Pres. So Allie and I would be alone with Kiki to do what we had to do—completely make her over into Talia French.

I paced by the club's pay phone, waiting for Ian to call me back. When the phone finally rang, I jumped for it.

"Hello?"

"We're in," Ian replied.

"Yes!" I cried, pumping the air with my fist. "What did you tell her?"

"I told her there would be one rehearsal, and that would be tonight. She said she wants twenty-five dollars extra for the rehearsal, and a guarantee that she'll get to talk to Graham."

"I thought she already knew your dad. I thought she was in one of his videos."

"She does," Ian replied. "And she came to some dumb party Polimar Records gave for Dad after the video was shot, which is where I met her. But I'm sure my dad doesn't remember her."

"Oh yeah?" I said. "So how come you did? And how did you get her phone number?"

"Oh, I sort of remembered her name and stuff," Ian said uncomfortably. "Or maybe she was sort of extra nice to me because she thought it would help her get to Dad."

"That's beat," I commented.

"Yeah, well, someday I'll be an even bigger star than he is, and then people will just call him Ian Templeton's father."

"You're absolutely right," I agreed. "Thanks a zillion, Ian."

"Becky! Oh, Becky!" Muffy Sue called, hurrying over to me as I hung up the phone. She had on a sweatshirt that read: AMERICA'S LITTLE MISS SWEETHEART. Subtle, huh?

"What is it, Muffy?"

"Muffy Sue, please," she corrected me. "I was thinking maybe I should sing for your mom. Would you like to hear me do 'Tomorrow' from the Broadway musical *Annie*?"

"Gee, Muffy Sue," I said with regret. "I'd love to, but . . . Liza needs me now." I ran back outside to the picnic tables where everyone was just finishing up lunch. Allie was talking with Pete Tilly again—her favorite thing to do, it seemed—and I caught her eye and gave her the thumbs-up sign.

"Okay, Becky, you set for free swim after lunch?" Liza asked me, checking her clipboard.

"Sure," I replied.

"After that Tori is going to lead a relay race in the back field," Liza said. "Dixie will have another group doing cheers and baton twirls, and you and Allie go supervise arts and crafts downstairs in the art room. Okay?"

"Fine," I assured her.

She grinned at me. "You're doing a great job, Becky. I just wanted you to know that."

I got a warm, terrific feeling all over when she said that. "Thanks," I said, grinning.

"Oh, one other thing I've been meaning to tell you," Liza continued. "About Jodie Graff—I've noticed that she hangs around you a lot. I'm sure you've noticed how small she is for her age."

I nodded. "She told me she's twelve, but that's hard to believe."

"She really is twelve," Liza said. "That's why she's in with the oldest kids. But she can't really keep up with them physically. She was born with a hole in her heart. And from what I hear they can't operate on her because there's something wrong with her lungs, too. I don't think the doctors think she'll live to be very old."

"Wow, that's awful!" I exclaimed.

I looked over at Jodie, who was sitting on a bench talking with Tori. "Should Jodie even be at camp?" I considered.

Liza shrugged. "I don't know. She's a distant relative of the Babbits or something, and it was their call. They're planning to tell everyone about Jodie at the staff meeting tomorrow. But I just wanted to mention it to you. She can't really run or swim or do any of that stuff. So if you could kind of take an interest in her—you know, encourage her in drama and music and stuff like that—I would really appreciate it."

"You got it," I told Liza.

"Thanks, Becky," she said with a grin and hurried off.

"Hey, do we have swim after lunch?" Allie asked, running over to me.

"Yeah," I confirmed. I was still looking over at Jodie who was trying to look bored with the world.

"Jodie," Allie said, shaking her head. "The kid keeps trying to bum cigarettes from everyone! I tried to tell her it was totally uncool."

I told Allie what Liza had just told me.

"So that's why she's so tiny," Allie realized. "She definitely shouldn't be smoking!"

I nodded in agreement. "Can you imagine having a hole in your heart?" I asked her with a shudder.

I looked over at Jodie again. And it occurred to me that some things were even worse than not having a mother.

*　　*　　*

"I'm playing *what*?" Kiki screeched.

"Our mother," I said again. "You're a famous stage and TV star named Talia French."

It was later that evening, and Kiki had shown up right on time. Dad was gone, Sam was gone, and everything was going according to plan. Until this.

"I can't play your mother," Kiki said. "I'm not nearly old enough to be your mother!"

Yeah, right. Her bags had bags.

"How old are you?" Allie asked her bluntly.

"Twenty-four," she said with a straight face.

If she was twenty-four, I was Julia Roberts. "Well, you're an actress," I reminded her. "Just *act* like you're about thirty-five," I suggested.

"So, what is this gig, anyway?" Kiki asked me. "Why am I supposed to pretend to be your mother?"

I looked over at Allie. She obviously expected me to run with the ball.

"Well, we're counselors at this camp," I explained slowly. "And, uh . . . Tuesday is Parents' Day. And, uh . . . we don't actually have a mother to bring."

Compassion suffused Kiki's overly made-up face. "Oh, you poor kids!"

"Look, it's no biggie," Allie insisted. "My brilliant sister over here told everyone that our mother was this big soap star, so we need you to pretend to be her."

Kiki threw her arms around me and hugged me so tight I thought I would suffocate. "There, there, now," she said. "Of course I'll do that for you. Why didn't you just explain all of this in the first place? Now, what is it you want me to do?"

I looked over the outfit she had on—skintight black Levi's with a low-cut sequined T-shirt. "Let's talk about clothes."

"I've got a great wardrobe," Kiki responded eagerly. "Just tell me what you want."

"Something . . . tasteful?" I suggested.

"Understated?" Allie added.

"In other words, lose the cleavage," I concluded.

"Well, sure," Kiki agreed, scribbling notes on a piece of paper. "How about a well-cut, off-white linen pantsuit with, say, a silk T-shirt in mauve. Off-white low-heeled ankle boots, my hair down but held off the face with two mother-of-pearl French combs, and the faintest trace of cosmetics?"

I was stunned. "That sounds perfect," I agreed. "Can you do that?"

"Darling, I'm an actress," Kiki assured me with dignity. "Of course I can do it."

"Well, that would be great!" I cried. "Perfect!" I was beginning to feel like this really was going to work out. I filled her in on Talia's career and then Allie and I told her all about ourselves, so she would know something about her "daughters."

"Great," Kiki said when we were through. "I think I've got it all down, and I'll study my notes before Tuesday. Anything else?"

Kiki Coors was rapidly improving in my judgment. "I can't think of anything," I replied.

She clicked her pen and stuck it in her purse along with her notes. "I was wondering," Kiki asked, "why isn't your dad going to this parent day thing?"

"He's going to be out of town," Allie explained. "That's why the coast is clear for you."

"You mean you two wouldn't have had a parent at Parents' Day at all?" Kiki asked sympathetically. "That's just so terrible!"

Just at that moment, I heard the front door open.

"Girls, I'm home!" Dad called from the hallway.

"Rats!" I whispered, quickly looking at my watch. "It's only seven-forty-five! What's he doing home from his date so early?"

"Girls? Where are you?" Dad called.

"In the family room," Allie called back.

We stared at each other, totally panicked.

"Julie wasn't feeling well," Dad was saying as he came toward the family room. "So we skipped the movie and I took her ho—"

Dad stopped dead in his tracks, staring at Kiki.

"Hello," Dad said, clearly wondering who the heck she was.

"Hello," Kiki replied, standing up.

"Uh, Dad, this is Kiki Coors," I said. "Kiki, this is our father, Dan Jacobs."

"Nice to meet you," my father said, shaking Kiki's hand. He gave us a questioning look.

"Kiki is an actress," I began. "She's a . . . a drama specialist at Club Sunset!"

Kiki nodded in agreement and sat back down.

"Are you now?" Dad asked with interest, sitting in the chair opposite us.

"She sure is," Allie agreed. "Boy, is she talented."

"Oh, well, I do my best," Kiki demurred.

"The girls didn't mention you were coming over," Dad said.

"Oh, I just stopped in and surprised them, Mr. Jacobs," Kiki improvised. "I have to tell you how truly talented your daughters are!"

"Please, call me Dan," my father urged her.

"Dan," Kiki said, smiling prettily. "I think they've both got big futures in show business. That's why I'm spending extra time with them!"

"Is that so?" Dan asked, clearly pleased.

"Well, girls, I won't take up any more of your time," Kiki said, getting up from the couch. "I just wanted to give you that information about the special camp play on Tuesday!"

My father got up quickly. "Please, don't feel you need to leave on my account!"

"Oh, I was only planning on a quick visit," Kiki replied. "I thought I'd catch that Meg Ryan movie at the Sunset Cinema."

"By yourself?" my father asked.

"Well, yes," Kiki said. "I don't mind, really. As an actress, I get to study the characters that way."

"It's the darnedest coincidence," my father said.

"But I was just heading over to the Meg Ryan movie when my friend got sick."

"No!" Kiki said, wide-eyed.

"It's true!" Dad replied. "I was wondering—I mean, if it wouldn't be too presumptuous—maybe you'd like some company?"

Kiki pretended to think a moment. "I think that would be lovely," she finally said.

Dad grinned happily. "Great!" He took Kiki by the elbow and led her to the doorway. "I'll see you girls later," he added.

They left. Allie and I sat there, totally stunned.

I had completely misjudged Kiki Coors. She was the best actress I had ever seen. And now she had a date with my father.

NINE

"Hi," Ethan said in a casual voice, as he moseyed over to us the next afternoon. The younger kids were playing kickball, and we were supervising and cheering them on. It was warm out, but the wind was fierce.

I was sitting in the front row of the bleachers with Allie and Dixie, and Tori was on the field coaching our team. We needed it. In the third inning we were behind, four to one.

Ethan put his hands in his pockets and rocked back on his heels. "So, how's it going?"

"Okay," I replied, keeping my eye on Kira, who was up at the plate next. Tori was demonstrating how to kick the ball without falling over, which is what had happened to Kira her first time up.

"Kick that ball! Kick that ball!" the red team chanted.

"Your team is going to kill you, coming over to the other side like this," Dixie chided Ethan, grinning warmly.

He smiled back. "I'll tell 'em I was spying on your

strategy or something," he replied, then ever-so-casually he sat down next to Dixie.

"What strategy?" I asked him. "We're losing."

He didn't even notice I'd said anything. He was too busy staring at Dixie.

"How are you liking camp so far?" Dixie asked him.

"It's okay," he said with a shrug.

"I saw you do that somersault dive at the pool yesterday," Dixie told him. "You were amazing!"

"No biggie," Ethan replied, but he looked like he was so happy he was going to levitate from joy.

Ethan and Dixie talked some more. He found an excuse to tug her hair, then he tickled her, and they wound up almost sort of kind of holding hands for a second there. Boy, did that make me miss Ian.

As for Allie, she had her eyes glued to Pete Tilly, who was coaching our team with Tori.

"He is so cute," Allie sighed.

"He's okay," I said.

"You know what he said today at lunch?" Allie continued. "That he wasn't surprised that our mother's a famous actress, because I'm so dramatic."

I made a face. "Are you sure that's good?"

"Well, yeah," Allie said. "I hope."

"I'm not feeling so terrific about good old Kiki," I told her, whispering so no one else could hear. A gust of wind blew my hair in my face, and I stuck it behind one ear. "Dad didn't get home until after midnight last night!"

She gave me a look. "You were awake?"

I nodded. "I couldn't sleep. And then this morning at breakfast he kept talking about how terrific she is and how he wants to see her again."

Allie looked alarmed. "I didn't hear that!"

"Because you spent the whole morning in the bathroom trying to get cute for Pete," I said with disgust.

"Dad's actually going to date Kiki *again*?" Allie asked, aghast.

I nodded. "He said they might go out to dinner tomorrow night. Saturday night. Official date night," I added significantly.

"Yuck," Allie replied. "Extreme and serious yuck."

Down on the field Kira was at the plate. The red team began to chant "Ki-ra! Ki-ra! Ki-ra!" She faced the ball.

A boy from the blue team rolled the ball to Kira. She pulled back her foot and kicked hard.

Zoom! The ball rolled fast past the pitcher. A shortstop went for it, but missed and tripped on her shoelaces.

"I've got it! I've got it!" Muffy Sue yelled, running from the outfield. Just then a strong gust of wind blew the ball past her. Muffy Sue was actually blown over, her frilly white shirt billowing over her head. She screamed and frantically tried to pull it down. Meanwhile, the ball scuttled across the field, the blue team kids running after it.

The red team went wild, yelling and cheering for

Kira to run around the bases. Allie, Dixie, and I jumped up, yelling and screaming, too.

Two little kids from the blue team ran after the ball, which had disappeared into the woods beyond the field. Kira rounded third base and headed for home.

"Run! Run!" we all screamed.

Kira pumped her little legs and crossed home plate while the kids were still retrieving the ball.

Allie and I ran down to join our team. Dixie followed and Ethan ambled back to his own team.

"You tied the game!" I told Kira, giving her a big hug.

"I runned so big!" she cried happily.

"I knew you could do it!" Shyla yelled, dancing around in a circle.

"Hey, that wasn't fair!" the pitcher from the blue team yelled. "The wind took the ball!"

"Crybaby! Crybaby!" a boy from our team taunted the pitcher.

I hit Tori in the arm. "You did great, Coach!"

"She's a terrific athlete, huh?" Pete said with a grin.

"Oh, well, I, uh . . ." Tori stammered.

Another giant gust of wind came up, practically knocking me over. The little kids were actually getting blown around.

"Hey, I think we're gonna need to call this game on account of the wind," Liza suggested.

"No way!" Greg cried. "You guys just tied the game! We need a chance to get our lead back!"

The wind gusted again and dark clouds gathered rapidly.

A whistle blew from behind us at the top of the bleachers. We turned and looked up, and there was Bobby Babbit. He had a megaphone with him. The wind was blowing his swirl of hair all over the place. It looked like a long, hairy snake was dancing around off of his bald, pink head. I bit my lip to keep from laughing.

"Liza, Greg," he called down, "you better bring the kids in. I don't like this weather! Bring them into the rec room downstairs and we'll play some games."

"Okay!" Liza called back. She turned to Greg. "You heard the man."

"Okay," Greg allowed, "but we'll finish this game on Monday."

Liza grinned at him wickedly. "You are just so competitive, Greg."

Liza turned to me. "Listen, can you junior C.I.T.s go down to the beach and check on the canoes and paddle boats? Make sure they're all secured before this storm hits."

"Sure," I agreed. I got Allie, Tori, and Dixie and we headed for the beach.

The wind was really whipping now, and the sky was darkening quickly.

"What am I going to do?" Tori moaned as we hurried to the beach. "I turn into an imbecile every

69

time Pete says anything to me!" She looked over at Dixie. "If your parents are so overprotective and everything, how come you never have any trouble talking to guys?"

Dixie shrugged. "I just pretend they're all judges at a beauty pageant," she replied. "You talk about what the judge wants to talk about and you act real charming, and then they're hooked!"

I laughed and shook my head. "You amaze me."

We crested the hill leading down to the beach. Out in the choppy, dangerous-looking water, I saw something. Some kind of boat, long and white, with two masts. It rocked crazily, as if it were going to capsize at any moment.

It was heading straight for Sunset Island.

TEN

"Look at that!" I cried, pointing out to the boat.

It was coming closer to shore. Though it was obviously some kind of a sailboat, none of the sails were up. Over the wind, I could hear some kind of motor on the boat. But to tell the truth it sounded a lot like my dad's car did once when we sprung an oil leak. Sick, you know?

"What should we do?" Tori asked.

None of us had an answer.

"Maybe it's a pirate ship, full of cute, young pirates who all look like Joey Lawrence," Allie fantasized.

"In your dreams," I snorted.

"Do you think we should go call someone?" Tori asked, ready to run back to the country club for help. "The Coast Guard, maybe?"

"It looks to me like the boat will be on shore before you could even make the phone call," Dixie pointed out. "Let's go down and see what's up."

We ran down the hill. The boat continued rocking

and reeling toward shore, pushed by the wind and the waves.

"Hey, there are a lot of people on that boat!" Tori exclaimed, squinting out at the ocean.

As the boat came closer I could make out fifteen or twenty people. And as it came closer still, I could see that they weren't just people. They were boys. Lots of cute boys. And they were all waving at us.

"Oh Tori," I singsonged, "this could be your lucky day."

"What do you mean?" she asked. "Those people could be in trouble! That boat is about to be grounded!" It was now only about thirty feet from shore. And then, with a couple of big waves, it was aground on the beach below us.

"Not so much," I said offhandedly, as I watched a couple of older guys hustling the boys off the bow, which by now was high and dry on the sand. "In fact, I have a feeling it's you who's in trouble, Tori."

"Why?" she asked me.

"Because Guy Paradise just landed at your feet!" I said with a laugh. I grinned at my sister and she grinned back.

"Tons of gorgeous guys!" Allie yelped. "I got my wish!"

Dixie looked dazzled. "Well, hush mah puppies," she drawled jokingly, "there's a whole lot of boys!"

Just then there was a huge clap of thunder. The sky was so dark it looked like dusk.

"Well, so what?" Tori asked, baffled.

"Tori babe," I said, imitating Sam. "Fifteen guys just washed up at our feet. Let's go get 'em!"

We ran over to the boat.

"Hi!" I yelled over the noise of the wind. "Can we help?"

"The motor quit!" one of the older guys yelled to me. "Too rough for the sails. Can you get me to a phone?"

"Sure," I said. "No problem. Where are you guys from?"

"Camp Eagle," the guy said. He looked to be college age, with sandy hair and big blue eyes. "I'm Randy, the head counselor. We were on a day trip."

An even louder clap of thunder startled me, and then lightning sizzled across the darkened sky.

"Some trip, huh?" a cute guy about my age said to me, shivering in his shorts and T-shirt. He was a little taller than me, with wavy brown hair and big brown eyes.

The guys helped us drag the Club Sunset boats farther up the beach. Just as we finished the sky broke loose and sheets of rain began to pour down on us.

"Follow me!" I yelled, and we ran back up the hill toward camp.

By the time we got there, we were all out of breath and soaking wet. Everyone from camp was in the huge main room, playing charades and duck-duck-goose. They all looked up when we walked in with all these guys.

"Look what we found on the beach!" I yelled. Then

I took Randy over to Barbi and Bobby, who were picking out music for the boom box at the front of the room.

"Is there some way these kids can dry off?" Randy asked Bobby.

"Oh, sure, man," Bobby said. "Pete!" he called. "Can you get some towels for these guys?"

"Sure, I'll get some from the pool," Pete said, trotting off.

"Okay, guys, just have a seat and we'll figure out what we're going to do," Randy told his campers. The cute guy smiled at me and sat down with his friends.

Randy turned back to Bobby. "We're not going to be able to get back to camp for a while," he explained. "This storm is a big one."

"Hey, no problem!" Bobby insisted, clapping Randy on the back. "We're happy to have you with us! You can hang for the day and we'll all kind of groove together!"

"Pssst," I hissed at my sister and my friends. "Come with me!" I grabbed my purse and we ran to the ladies' room. "Emergency repairs!" I told them.

"For what?" Tori asked, confused.

"Tori, do you want to look like a drowned rat in front of all those guys?" I prodded.

"Who cares?" she retorted. "I'm wash and wear!"

"Hey, consider this your first lesson in boys," I told her. "Stick your head under that hot-air dryer."

Tori rolled her eyes, but she did what I told her to

74

do. I fluffed her hair while she squatted down, turning her head under the stream of air.

As soon as Tori's hair was dry, Dixie posed under the dryer. Meanwhile, the rest of us put on a little lipstick and mascara. Except Tori.

"I hate makeup!" she exclaimed.

"Allie and I are the guy experts," I admonished. "You may never have another opportunity like this in your life. Fifteen guys just got stranded with you for the day."

She sighed and held still while I put a faint touch of lipstick on her lips.

"I don't know why I'm bothering," Tori said. "I won't be able to talk to those guys anyway."

"Pretend you're Dixie," Allie advised. "Pretend they're judges and you're in a beauty pageant."

Tori made a face. "No offense, Dixie, but that makes me want to blow major chunks. First of all, I hate beauty pageants, and second of all, I'm not sitting around waiting for guys to judge me. Yuck!"

Dixie laughed. "It's okay. How about this. Just picture the guy you're talking to doing some basic thing that will make him seem more human to you."

"Like what?" Tori pressed. "Eating? Spitting?" Her face reddened. "Bodily functions?"

"Okay, forget that advice," I said quickly. "How about if you pretend the guy is a girl? In other words, just talk to him like you talk to us."

She didn't look convinced, but we couldn't stay in the bathroom forever. So we picked up our stuff and headed back to the main room.

"Follow me," I muttered to my friends, and led them over to the guys from Camp Eagle.

"Hi," I said, sitting down next to the cute brown-haired guy. "I'm Becky. And this is my sister Allie, and this is Dixie, and Tori.

"Twins, cute!" he said, his eyes lighting up. "I'm Dave Kravitz," he continued, flashing me that cute grin again. "This is Larry, Tim, and A.J.," he added, indicating the guys sitting near him.

I looked his friends over quickly. Larry was short with blond hair, bad skin, and braces. Tim had dark, curly hair and was built like an athlete, and A.J. was tall and skinny, with a very handsome face and long brown hair tied back in a ponytail. He was wearing a tie-dyed Save The Whales T-shirt. The other three guys had on white Camp Eagle T-shirts.

"What's A.J. stand for?" Dixie asked the tall guy.

"Aquarius Jeff," Dave replied for his friend. "Because he's into all that hippie dippie, new age stuff."

A.J. grinned good-naturedly. "It's really Arnold Jeffrey," he admitted. "So A.J. is a lot better, don't you think?"

"Arnold!" his friends called nasally, holding their noses shut. "Arnold!"

A.J. laughed. "Ignore these buttheads," he advised. "The only reason they can get away with this is because we've known each other since we were in kindergarten."

"Yeah, and A.J. was all nature-boy'd out even then!" Tim teased him.

"Are you guys counselors or what?" Allie asked.

"Senior campers," Larry said. "We're all fourteen, going into ninth. At Eagle you're a camper until you're sixteen."

"Cool," I replied. "You don't have to work. We do!"

We talked a while longer. All four guys lived in Portland and their families had summer houses on Eagle Island. Dave seemed to be the leader and was going to be president of the ninth grade class that upcoming year. Tim was probably the cutest in a jock-preppie kind of way, and was on every sports team there was.

"Tori is a great athlete, too," I said, nudging Tori forward.

"Yeah?" Tim asked her. "What's your sport?"

"I . . . uh, well—" Tori stammered.

"All sports!" Dixie answered for her.

"So, what's your favorite?" Tim asked.

Tori gulped. "Baseball," she managed in a low voice.

Tori and Tim began talking about sports. She was actually carrying on a conversation! I went over to see if Liza needed any help with the kids. When I came back, Allie was talking with Dave and Dixie was deep in conversation with A.J.

I sat down next to Larry. He was pulling something gross out of his braces.

"These stupid things are killing my mouth," he complained. "I just got them on last week."

"Hurts, huh?" I asked him.

"Yeah, they hurt me and my girlfriend, too," he replied. "I just about chewed her lips off last night."

Oh, I guess this was his way of telling me he was making out with his girlfriend the night before. Like I could care.

"Okay, guys, here's the plan," Randy said, coming over to us. "This storm isn't supposed to let up until some time late tonight or tomorrow. There are gale-force winds and tornado warnings. In other words, we're going to be here for a while."

"That's okay," Dave said, looking over at me quickly.

I smiled at him. He was *very* cute.

By the time I remembered about Ian, it was too late to take that smile back.

ELEVEN

The weather got even worse and we would all be stuck at camp until cars could get down the roads to the country club. Outside we could hear the wind howling. Rain slapped sideways against the building. It was scary and wonderful at the same time.

Not that my friends or I minded the situation. We were getting along great with Dave, Tim, Larry, and A.J., and they helped us out with the kids. Some of the kids were scared and started crying. Dave took two boys who were especially scared on a walk around the upstairs level of the country club, and when they came back the kids were smiling.

Dixie and A.J. paired off, as did Tori and Tim. Dave, Larry, Allie, and I hung together.

When I got Allie alone I asked her about Dave.

"You like him?" I probed.

"Yeah, he's cute," she replied. "Why? You don't like him, do you?"

"He seems nice," I said. "I mean as a friend. I have a boyfriend."

"The whole world knows you have a boyfriend," Allie said. "So, no problem, right?"

"Right," I agreed, but I had this funny feeling inside, like I didn't want Allie to be with Dave. That was nuts, wasn't it?

We fed the kids dinner, and then the older counselors took them into another room where they spread blankets and sleeping bags out on the floor. Liza and Greg arranged a rotating schedule for us to watch the kids. A.J. and Tim volunteered to take the first shift with Tori and Dixie.

Back in the main room, Bobby and Barbi put on some old rock music and camp turned into a huge party. We ate hot dogs and burgers and the older counselors started to dance.

"A.J. would probably love this music," Dave said. "The guy is stuck in a time warp!"

"What kind of music do you like?" Allie asked him.

"Oh, you know, Pearl Jam, some metal, some alternative," he replied. He looked over at me. "You wanna dance?"

"Okay," I said casually, like it didn't mean anything.

We danced to an old Beatles song. Larry and Allie danced next to us. Now the older campers were getting up to dance, too. Only Jodie seemed to hang by herself at a table. Then I remembered that she couldn't dance because of her heart. Before I could do anything, though, Pete Tilly went over and sat with her.

When the song ended, a ballad came on. Dave raised his eyebrows at me, like, did I want to slow dance. I moved into his arms.

Out of the side of my eyes, I could see Allie giving me dirty looks. I ignored her. It felt great to have Dave's arms around me. He smelled good, too. As soon as the song ended, Allie grabbed my arm and dragged me into the hall.

"What's the deal?" she asked me.

"What?"

"I thought you only liked him as a friend," she said.

"Yeah, and . . . ?"

"And you don't slow dance with your friends," she warned. "I got stuck with Larry who keeps talking about his girlfriend and how perfect she is."

"Well, I can't help it if Dave asked me to dance!" I protested.

Allie folded her arms. "I bet he can't even tell us apart, right?"

"I guess," I agreed.

"So, if you really loved me, you'd go in the bathroom with me and switch clothes. Then he'll think I'm you and he'll ask me to dance."

"We don't need to do that," I protested. "I'll just tell him about Ian."

Allie cocked her head to one side. "You'd do that?"

"Of course," I said. "I love Ian."

"Gross," Allie commented. "Don't you think you're a little young to be in love?"

"No," I replied.

Tori came running over from her babysitting post. "Quick! I have to talk to you! Before Tim gets back from the john!"

"We're supposed to go in with the little kids," Allie said.

"I'm not on for another half hour," I reminded her, "I'm supposed to go put the games away."

"Oh, and I guess Dave is going to help you," Allie added, her hands on her hips.

"Well, he offered."

She shot me a dark look. "Don't do anything I wouldn't do," she huffed before leaving.

"So, do you like Tim?" I asked Tori.

"He's wonderful!" she said, her eyes shining. "I mean, he's really nice, and he does all the sports I do, and he's a Red Sox fan just like me!"

"So, great!" I encouraged her. "Soon you'll move on to locking lips, and then he's yours!"

"Are you kidding?" Tori hissed. "Never! He probably doesn't like me like that!"

"Sure he does!" I insisted.

She grabbed the sleeve of my T-shirt. "They're *dancing* in the other room!" she cried.

"And?"

"And I can't dance!" Tori cried.

"Of course you can dance. You're an athlete!"

"What if I trip? What if I fall? What if the music gets slow and he wants to slow dance and I get close to him and I have bad breath? What if I—"

"This is the greatest day of my life," Dixie interrupted, running over to us. "Isn't A.J. the sweetest guy in the world?" She saw how white Tori looked. "What's wrong?"

"They're *dancing* in there!" she yelped.

"I know," Dixie said happily. "I love to dance! And my parents aren't here to make sure there's daylight between me and the boy I'm dancing with!"

"But I can't dance!" Tori protested.

"Oh, sure you can," Dixie said easily. "All you need to do is move to the music."

"I can't!" Tori insisted, looking miserable. "I'm missing the dancing gene or something!"

Just then Tim and A.J. came back from the john and Dave and Larry came out to join us.

"Hey, we heard about your mom," Tim said.

"It's no big deal," I said. "I don't even miss her that much. I mean, I was so little when she went away and everything."

Everyone was looking at me strangely.

"She's been acting in New York since you were a baby?" A.J. asked.

Oh, shoot! I had completely forgotten about Talia French, a.k.a. Kiki Coors.

"Oh, I meant she's been a famous actress since I was little," I explained quickly. "I mean it isn't weird to me to have her gone sometimes, what with her being so famous and all, is what I meant," I babbled.

"My sister loves that soap 'Forever Young,' Tim

said. "She just had a baby, so she quit her job to stay home with the kid. And she watches that thing every single day."

"Mom's not on the show right now," I explained.

"So, she's gonna be here Tuesday, right?" A.J. asked. "That's what Dixie said."

"Right," I agreed. "Boy, I can't wait to see Mom."

"Becky, did you put away the kids' toys?" Liza asked, walking briskly down the hall.

"No, I was just going to do that."

"Now would be a good time," she suggested, hurrying by me.

"I'll come help you," Dave offered.

"Let's go dance!" Dixie suggested to the others.

Tori gave me one final look of panic, and then headed into the main room with the others.

Dave and I went to the playroom and started picking up the Legos, puzzle pieces, and building blocks that were scattered everywhere.

"Picking up after little kids is a pain, huh?" I said.

"It's not so bad," Dave commented, dropping a bunch of puzzle pieces into a box. "I've got two little sisters, so I've done a lot of this."

I snuck a look at him as I piled some red Lego pieces into a toy chest. Why was I so attracted to him? Usually I liked guys who seemed tough, wore leather jackets, and didn't care about school. Or I liked guys like Ian, the true artist types. But Dave wasn't either of those. He was clean-cut, a good student, and a nice guy.

He was—gasp!—someone my father would approve of.

"So, how long have you been going to Camp Eagle?" I asked him, scraping some Play-Doh off a table.

"My whole life practically," Dave said. "I started when I was five. My dad went there when he was a kid."

"No kidding."

"Yeah," Dave said. "It's like this family tradition, or something. I'll probably go back as a counselor when I'm sixteen." He stacked up some plastic chairs in the corner. "You like camp?"

"It's okay," I said. "I mean, I like the kids. But I suppose it can be a drag, too." I got a sponge and started to clean off the tables.

"So, do you guys have, like, parties and stuff?" Dave asked casually.

"I don't know," I said honestly. "We just started camp this week."

"We're having a dance next Friday night," Dave said. "It's only for age fourteen and up. Some of the guys invite girls who aren't at camp. It should be okay."

I nodded and my heart beat a little faster. Was this going where I thought this was going?

"So, I thought maybe you'd like to go," he said, not looking at me.

Yes, yes, yes! I *definitely* wanted to go!

But I couldn't. There was Ian. I was in love with Ian. And there was Allie.

"Gee, I'd really like to come," I told Dave. "But the thing is, I have a boyfriend."

"Oh yeah?"

I nodded again. "You could ask Allie," I added.

He laughed. "Why, you think that just because you look kind of alike you're interchangeable?"

"Yeah," I replied honestly.

"Well, you're not. I just met the two of you and I can already see that you're totally different."

"Different how?" I asked. No one had ever said this to me before.

"You're nicer and more cheerful and more energetic. You're kinder to the little kids. You're more outgoing. And you're prettier, too."

I put my hands on my hips. Now I knew he was teasing me. "Oh, yeah, sure," I sniffed. "You can't tell us apart. No one can."

"I can," he said in a low voice.

"You mean the stupid mole?" I asked him.

He walked over to me. Then he took his finger and ever-so-gently touched me right over my lip. "This isn't a mole. It's a beauty mark."

I blushed, my face going all hot. I felt as dumbstruck and breathless as Tori.

"Besides," he added, "your eyes are different."

"They are?" I asked in a soft voice.

"Yep," he said. "It's the first thing I noticed about you."

Then slowly he leaned toward me. It's like I was hypnotized. I just couldn't seem to stop myself.

I raised my face to his.

TWELVE

"Yo, Becky! Liza wants to know where you put the videos the kids were watching yesterday," Tori bellowed, stomping into the playroom.

Dave and I jumped apart. But not before Tori saw us together, just about to kiss.

Her face turned the color of the "stop" signal on a traffic light.

"Oh, I'm sorry!" she cried, backing toward the doorway. "I mean, I didn't mean to . . . I mean, oh, wow, well, uh, gee, I—"

"It's okay," I finally interrupted her. "Forget about it."

"Well, don't I feel like the hind end of a donkey," she joked as her back hit the door. "Dumb old me! Okay, I'm gone. I'm outta here!"

"Look, it's no big thing," Dave called to her.

"I didn't see a thing, I swear!" she yelled back to us, already out the door.

The mood was broken. And I realized that the last thing I should be doing at that moment was kissing this guy in the playroom at camp.

"Well, like I said," I told Dave, reaching for a puzzle piece we'd missed, "I have a boyfriend."

"You sure?" Dave asked me.

"Yeah," I said, but I couldn't meet his gaze. "Listen, I should get back . . ."

"We can be friends, can't we?" Dave asked.

"Oh, sure!" I agreed. One part of me was relieved that he was being so nice about it and another part of me was ticked off that he wasn't putting up more of a fight.

Dave went into the main room and I went to take my turn watching the kids. Most of them were asleep, but Shyla and Kira were awake, sitting in the corner with Jodie. She was telling them a story, in her low, grown-up voice.

". . . So then the big monster turned to the little girl and said 'I'm going to eat you up.' But the little girl said 'No way, monster,' and she used her magic powers to turn the monster into a big pile of mud. She stepped in the mud on her way to the White House, where she was about to become the first six-year-old female president of the United States, and she lived happily ever after."

"That's a great story!" Shyla said. "Did the little girl have brown skin or white skin?"

"Both," Jodie replied without missing a beat. "She could, like, change her skin color with her magic powers, too."

"I wish I could do that," Kira said, snuggling

sleepily against Jodie. "I would like to be same color as Shyla."

"I'd like to be multicolored myself," Jodie said. The little girls both giggled. "Can you guys sleep now?"

The girls nodded and they settled down on their sleeping bags.

"That was pretty cool," I told Jodie when she came over to the doorway.

She shrugged. "Your sister went to the john or something, so I said I'd hang in here for a while."

"Thanks," I told her in a whisper. "You can go back to the party now if you want to."

"What I really want is a cigarette," she complained.

"Maybe you should get that nicotine patch thing," I suggested. "Isn't that supposed to help people stop smoking?"

She rolled her eyes at me. "Who says I want to stop?"

"Well, it's really bad for you."

She shrugged again. "Hey, live fast, die young, I always say. See ya." She walked away.

I watched her go. I didn't think she meant what she said about dying young. I didn't like to think about what it would be like to be her.

Allie came back and walked over to me. "How's Dave?"

"He's okay," I said. We sat down on a table, dangling our legs over the edge.

"So, did you tell him about Ian?"

I nodded.

She looked surprised. "Wow, you really are in love with Ian, huh?"

"I told you I was. So if you want to go for Dave, it's fine with me."

"Nah," she said. "He's too young. I think I want Pete Tilly."

"Whatever," I replied. But in my heart, I was glad Allie didn't want Dave. It didn't make any sense, but that's how I felt.

Liza stuck her head in the doorway. "Hey, the storm is finally letting up," she whispered. "We're gonna wake the kids in a little bit. But if you guys want to call home, someone can come get you in about forty-five minutes."

"I'll go call," I offered to Allie. I went out into the hall and dropped a quarter into the pay phone.

"Hello?" came my father's voice.

"Hi, Dad, it's Becky."

"Sweetheart! Is everything okay there?"

"Yeah," I replied. "Liza says the storm is letting up, so Sam can pick us up in, like, forty-five minutes."

"Sam got stuck at Emma's when the storm hit, so she's not back yet. But Kiki and I could come and get you."

I couldn't have heard him correctly. "What did you say?" I asked.

"Your drama specialist friend from camp," Dad explained jovially. "She came over earlier, and then the storm hit. We've been having a really cozy evening."

"I'll bet," I mumbled.

"Lucky for me there wasn't any drama going on at camp today, huh?" Dad asked.

"Yep, that's lucky all right," I replied.

His voice got lower. "She's really great, Becky."

"Gee, that's just . . . swell," I offered.

"So, Kiki and I will see you in a little while," Dad said. "Bye!"

"Allie!" I wailed, running back to find her. "You are not going to believe this!" I pulled her into the hallway and filled her in.

"They're together?" she screeched. "They're a *couple*!? That's completely disgusting!"

"What if someone sees her in the car when they show up to pick us up?" I hissed. "Our whole plan will be wrecked!"

"Not if we jump into the car and no one talks to her," Allie calculated. "If anyone sees her with Dad today, it'll just be that much more authentic when they see her on Tuesday!"

I held my stomach. "I have a bad feeling about this. What if she wears one of her sleazy outfits? What if she shows up here in a shirt cut down to her navel?"

"That would be completely mortifying," Allie agreed. "Okay, we'll just have to be waiting down near the parking lot when they get here, so Dad

93

doesn't even have to bring the car up to the front of the building."

"Yeah, that's a plan," I agreed.

Liza and Pete rounded the corner. "The buses will be here in fifteen minutes," they said. "And we just got a call from Camp Eagle that the ferry is running, so a van's coming for their kids."

We got the kids up and ready to go. Some parents showed up; the other kids got shepherded into the waiting buses. When the kids were gone, I was surprised to find it was past ten o'clock at night. I walked over to an exhausted Liza.

"Thanks, Becky," she said. "Boy, am I glad this day is over."

"So am I." I turned to go back into the building, and there was Dave.

"So, it was really great to meet you and everything," he said.

"Same here," I agreed.

"I was wondering if I could call you," he continued. "Just as a friend," he added quickly.

"That would be okay," I agreed nonchalantly. He wrote my phone number on a slip of paper and stuck it in his pocket. Then he leaned over and quickly kissed me on the lips. "See ya," he said, and then he hurried off to the Camp Eagle van.

Tori came running over to me. "Tim asked for my phone number!" she screeched, grabbing my hand.

"That's great!" I assured her. "I knew he liked you!"

94

"Maybe he doesn't really," she said, suddenly looking worried. "Maybe he just wants to talk about sports or something."

I looked over at the Camp Eagle van, and there was Dixie talking with A.J. And they were holding hands. He brushed some hair off her face and slowly pulled away from her and reluctantly got into the van. Dixie sort of floated over to us.

"Y'all, my whole life is changed," she drawled in this blissed out voice.

"I guess that means you like him," I said.

"He invited me to a dance at their camp next Friday night!" Dixie cried, hugging herself.

Tori looked crestfallen. "Gee, Tim didn't say anything about that."

"Maybe he's going to call and invite you," I said.

"No, never," she determined. "He only likes me as a friend. I know that's it."

"Do you know that A.J. doesn't eat meat?" Dixie asked us dreamily. "He says he can't eat any living thing with a soul. Isn't that beautiful?"

"Yeah, sure," I agreed. But my mind wasn't really on what she was saying. I was watching the Camp Eagle van pull away, knowing Dave was in it.

Just as the van was turning out of the parking lot I saw Dave's face in the van's window, illuminated by the lights that surrounded the country club. His eyes caught mine and he put his hand up to the window, as if he wanted to be touching my hand.

I had to snap out of it.

I turned back to my friends.

"Oh, Darcy's here," Dixie said, as Darcy and Molly drove up in Molly's van. "I'll call you later!" She was giving Tori a ride, so she and Tori hurried off.

Allie came out of the country club with Pete, laughing as if Pete had just said something truly hilarious.

In the distance I saw Dad's BMW pull down the private road near the parking lot. "Hey, Allie!" I called to her. "Let's book!"

She waved to Pete and ran over to me. Then we ran to the car so we could stop Dad and Kiki before they reached the camp.

"You didn't need to run down here," Dad said as we got into the backseat.

"That's okay," I said.

"Hi, girls," Kiki said, a friendly smile on her face.

"Hi," Allie said in a flat voice. "Imagine seeing you here."

"It's great to see you, too," Kiki said. "I bet you two are really tired, huh?"

"No," I replied obstinately. "In fact, Allie and I are probably going out with our friends tonight."

Dad turned the corner onto Beach Road. "Isn't it kind of late for that, girls?"

"No," I said bluntly. "It's Friday night."

"Well, I think it would be a good idea for you girls to just stay in," Dad said. "It's already after ten o'clock."

"I agree," Kiki said. "You girls had a tough day and you need some rest."

Allie and I both just sat there with our jaws open.

How could this be happening?

The actress we had hired to pretend to be our mother was dating our father and *telling us what to do!*

Aghhhhhhh!

THIRTEEN

It was a nightmare.

Dad and Kiki spent the entire weekend together.

Saturday night, when Allie and I left with Sam to go to the movies, Dad and Kiki were sitting cozily on the couch in front of some stupid movie they had rented.

Right before we left Kiki called out, "Get in by a reasonable hour, girls."

I considered murder a viable option.

Sunday Dad decided we should go on a family picnic. Suddenly, Kiki was part of this event. Her idea of cool clothes to wear for a picnic consisted of skintight cutoffs over a low-cut, shocking-pink bodysuit. Her lipstick was the same neon color as her top. Nail polish, too. Oh, and false eyelashes. To a picnic! When Dad saw her, he got this incredibly dumb look on his face, and it dawned on me that *he thought she looked good*.

It is a terrible thing to discover you have been raised by a person with no taste.

My first chance to be alone with Kiki came when Dad and Allie were taking a walk on the beach.

"You didn't eat very much," Kiki said to me, dropping some used paper plates into a garbage bag.

"No offense, but being around you is kind of making me lose my appetite." I couldn't believe it. She actually looked hurt. "Look, I don't know what your game is, but after Tuesday this stupid thing has to end," I told her.

"What stupid thing is that?" Kiki asked me.

"What, I have to paint you a picture? You are an actress, remember? We are hiring you to pretend to be our mother. You are not *actually* our mother. Does that ring a bell?"

Kiki took a handful of grapes and dropped one into her mouth. "I know I'm not your mother, Becky," she said.

"Well, good," I replied. "That means you still have some grasp on reality. And by the way, try to remember to wear the conservative outfit on Tuesday," I added, taking in her low-cup top.

"You can just cut the sarcasm out, okay?" Kiki said, popping another grape into her mouth. "Your dad and I like each other. One thing has nothing to do with the other."

I snorted back a laugh. "Please."

She cocked her head to one side, "Becky, you and Allie are really nice kids. And your dad is a great guy. I just happen to like all of you. That isn't a crime." She reached out and gently touched my hand.

I snatched it away. "We don't need you, and we don't want to be with you," I told her. "And if my dad knew who you really were, he wouldn't want to be with you either."

Kiki looked like she was ready to cry. For a moment I felt bad that I was being so awful to her. Then I remembered that she was an actress and she was only being nice to us for money.

Now didn't *that* sound familiar.

Monday everyone at camp was talking about how excited they were to meet my famous mother the next day.

"What should I wear?" Muffy Sue asked me as the campers and staff assembled on the playground for morning announcements.

"For what?" I asked her, not really paying attention to what she was saying.

"To meet your mother tomorrow!" she reminded me. "Golly, this could change my career!"

I stopped and looked at her. "What career? You're seven years old."

"So?" Muffy Sue asked. "Haven't you ever heard of child stars? Do you think if I wear my crown kids will think I'm showing off?"

"It's a good bet," I replied.

Dixie ran over to me and grabbed my hands. "He called me!"

"A.J.?" I asked her.

"Twice!" she cried. "I talked to a boy on the phone!"

Allie caught up with us and overheard Dixie. "Is that like a major news bulletin?"

"Yes!" Dixie replied. "I am not allowed to have boys call me at home! Once that boy from church called me, and my dad got on the extension and breathed as loud as he could. Then when I got off the phone he said boys can't call me until I'm sixteen."

"Dixie, that's very bizarre," I told her.

"I know," she agreed. "It's a wonder I haven't rebelled and run away from home or something. But being here for the summer is sort of like the same thing, isn't it? Y'all, I am so happy!"

Tori waved from the other side of the field and walked over to us. "Morning," she said glumly.

"What's up?" I asked her.

"Nothing," she replied. "Tim didn't call me. I knew he wouldn't. I don't know why I'm depressed about it. It's dumb. I probably had gunk on my teeth or something, and then when he looked at my mouth up close when we were slow dancing, he got totally grossed out."

"But A.J. told me Tim really likes you!" Dixie insisted.

"You told me that on the phone last night, Dixie," Tori reminded her. "But I don't see Tim picking up the phone." She shoved her hands deep into her oversized red shorts. "I am a guy-failure. That's just the way it is."

"I told you," I said, "you can always call him." This was advice I had gotten from Sam, and she knew everything about guys, so I figured it had to be right.

"I would never have the nerve in a zillion years," Tori admitted. "I mean, I'd have to have a really good reason to call him."

"I've got it!" Dixie cried. "Remember how Tim said his older sister watched 'Forever Young'? Well, you can get an autographed picture of Becky and Allie's mom for his sister! Now, that would be a great reason to call him!"

Tori looked hopeful. "Yeah, maybe . . ."

"It's perfect!" Dixie insisted. She turned to me and Allie. "Isn't it?"

"Gee, I don't know if Mom will have any photos with her—" I demurred.

"Well, you said she's not flying in until late today," Dixie reminded me. "You could call her and ask her to bring some!"

Tori and Dixie stared expectantly at me and Allie.

"Sure," I finally said, because I couldn't think of a way out of it. "I'll do that."

Great. I would be passing out photos of Kiki Coors, which she'd have to sign "Talia French." I just hoped good old Kiki wasn't wearing something gross like a thong bikini in her publicity shots.

Ring! Ring!
It was early the next morning. Parents' Day. I had

103

been sound asleep, but woke up to the ringing of the telephone on my nightstand.

"Go away!" Allie mumbled and pulled the pillow over her head.

I reached over and groggily answered the phone.

"Hi, it's Ian," came my boyfriend's voice.

"Oh hi," I said, and cleared my sleep-filled throat. "Why are you calling so early?"

"To wish you luck on the big day," Ian said. "I am definitely going to write a song about this. So, call me afterwards and tell me what happened, okay?"

"Yeah, I will," I promised.

"And remind Allie we have a Zits band practice tomorrow night," Ian added. "We'll try the new song out. This could be the one that gets us the record deal."

I said good-bye and hung up. Then I stared at the ceiling for a few minutes, praying that everything would go okay.

"You girls awake?" Dad asked, sticking his head into the room. He was carrying his small suitcase and was dressed in khaki pants and a golf shirt. "I wanted to kiss you good-bye."

"Have a good time, Dad," I said.

He came over and sat on the edge of my bed. "Something is bothering me, honey," he said. "I was talking to Jeff Hewitt on the golf course yesterday, and he told me that today is some kind of Parents' Day at your camp."

Uh-oh.

"I thought about not mentioning it to you girls," he continued. "But, well, it's bothering me. Did you not want your old dad there or something?"

"Oh, it's nothing like that," I insisted. "It's just that this is only for the little kids."

Allie sat up and watched us from across the room.

"Jeff mentioned that he and his wife, Jane, were both going," Dad said. "And Ethan is the same age as you guys, isn't he?"

"He's barely thirteen," Allie said quickly. "And . . . he's really, ah . . . immature," I lied.

Dad stood up looking kind of sad. "Well, if you're sure."

"Absolutely," I insisted.

He bent down and kissed my forehead and then went over to kiss Allie. "You girls be good," he said. "Listen to Sam. I'll be home Thursday evening. I'll miss you."

Finally he was gone.

"Whoa, we barely escaped total disaster," I said to Allie, jumping out of bed.

"With Kiki playing our mother, we may be heading into total disaster," Allie pointed out. "And it will be all your fault."

"We're in this together," I said stubbornly.

"Yeah, yeah," Allie grumbled.

"Whatever happens?" I asked her.

"Whatever happens," she agreed with resignation.

"Pinkie on it," I insisted.

She looked like she could kill me, but she held up her pinkie and touched mine.

When push comes to shove, I can always count on my sister.

"Girls!" Kiki cried, running over to us. "My darling girls!"

"Mom!" Allie and I both cried back, holding out our arms.

We were standing on the playground, where the campers gathered every morning. Parents were everywhere, but it felt as if all eyes were on Kiki as she ran over to embrace us.

The good news was she had on the tasteful, off-white suit, as planned. The bad news was she had on too much makeup and dangly earrings, but I guess you can't have everything.

When she embraced us in her suffocating manner, I whispered in her ear, "Don't act so excited. You were supposed to have arrived last night."

She held Allie and me at arms' length. "I know I saw you two darlings last night," she said in a loud voice, "but I love you so much I'm just thrilled to see you again!"

"Don't overdo it," Allie told her through the fixed smile on her face.

Kiki hooked her arms through Allie's and mine. "Now, I want to meet all your little friends!"

"Excuse me, Miss French?" Muffy Sue said, coming up to us. She had on a frilly white dress and tap shoes. No crown.

"Yes?" Kiki said.

"May I have your autograph?" Muffy Sue asked, wide-eyed.

"Darling, of course," Kiki said. She opened her large purse and took out a publicity shot of herself, which fortunately didn't have her name on it. She got out a pen and wrote, "Much love, Talia French" with a flourish.

"Thank you so much," Muffy Sue said. "I've seen you on TV a lot of times, and you are my favorite actress."

Yeah, right. Seven years old and already a stone-faced liar.

"Isn't that sweet?" Kiki purred.

"I'm going to tap dance in the talent show this afternoon," Muffy Sue informed Kiki. "I don't usually do amateur things, but you're here so it's different." She leaned close. "I'm America's Little Miss Sweetheart. I just didn't wear my crown. Tap is my talent."

"Great, sweetie," Kiki said. "I'll see you later."

"What an obnoxious child," Kiki said so no one but Allie and me could hear, a bright smile on her face.

Tori and Dixie came shyly over to us. I introduced them to "Mom."

"It's a real pleasure to meet you, ma'am," Dixie said.

"Oh no, you make me feel ancient!" Kiki cried with a laugh. "You must call me Tamala!"

Dixie looked confused.

"She means Talia," I said quickly. "It used to be Tamala, but . . . she changed it!"

"Right!" Allie agreed. "She changed it!"

"Wow, a famous person!" Tori cried. "I never met one before!"

Kiki laughed. "You two are so darling!" she gushed.

"If it wouldn't be too much trouble, we'd like autographed pictures of you," Dixie said shyly.

"No trouble at all," Kiki insisted, and took out two photos which she signed and handed to Dixie and Tori.

"Well, this must be the famous Ms. French," Bobby Babbit said, hurrying over to us with Barbi. "We're Bobby and Barbi Babbit, the camp directors. It's so groovy to have you here at Club Sunset!" He smoothed his swirly hair down on his scalp carefully, beaming at Kiki.

"Thank you so much," Kiki said graciously. "It's a pleasure to be here. But, please, I don't want any special attention while I'm here. I'm just happy to be here with my darling daughters."

Barbi looked from Kiki to me and Allie. "You know, you two girls look so much like your mom, it's really far-out!"

"Yes, everyone says that," Kiki agreed happily.

"Well, just make yourself comfortable," Bobby

said. "Peace and love!" He actually gave her the peace sign and he and Barbi hurried off to greet other parents.

"Aren't they . . . nice," Kiki said.

"Seriously stuck in the sixties," I explained.

Allie, Dixie, Tori, and I laughed, and Kiki laughed with us. "They are, aren't they?" she said.

"You should hear the music he makes us listen to!" Dixie exclaimed. "For the talent show this afternoon he and Barbi are doing a duet of 'Let the Sunshine In'!"

"Oh great," Tori groaned. "My parents will be here by then. They'll probably stand up and dance in the aisles."

We were all laughing, and I was feeling great. Kiki was actually pulling this off! A few more kids came over to us, including Jodie and some of the younger kids. Kiki was gracious to everyone. When people asked about her career, she was able to make up great lies on the spot. I have to say I was impressed.

Then, just as we were about to head to the campfire area where morning announcements always took place, I saw a terrible sight out of the corner of my eye.

It couldn't be true. But it was.

There was my father. Heading right toward us.

FOURTEEN

"Dad!" I cried.

"Girls!" Dad exclaimed.

"Dan!" Kiki yelled.

"Dad!" Allie repeated.

"Girls!" Dad said again.

We all just stood there staring at each other. Tori and Dixie looked benignly at our happy family unit.

My life was over.

"What are you *doing* here!?" I asked my father through my fixed smile.

"You know, I got to the airport and I just felt so darned bad about not being here with you girls on Parents' Day," my father said. "I know you said it was basically for the little kids, but it just didn't feel right. So I changed my flight to tonight, turned around, and drove right back here."

"That is so sweet!" Dixie exclaimed.

"Yeah, isn't it?" I said. I quickly introduced my father to Tori and Dixie.

"It's always nice to meet my daughters' friends,"

Dad said. Then he gave Kiki a shy smile. "It's nice to see you."

"Oh, well, nice to see you, too," Kiki said merrily. I could see the sweat starting to break out on her forehead.

"Will I get a chance to see any of the dramatic things you're working on with the kids here at camp?" he asked her.

Dixie and Tori looked confused.

"Oh, no time for that," I cried. "Hey, we better get over to the group now," I added, kind of pushing Tori and Dixie along.

"Oh, come on," Dad said with a laugh. "No need to be so modest! Kiki told me you guys are doing some really exciting stuff here!"

Please, just let the ground open up so that I can fall into a big pit and never be heard from again, I prayed. Unfortunately, that didn't happen. The ground stayed grounded, and Tori and Dixie were getting extremely suspicious.

"Kiki?" Tori asked.

"A pet name!" I cried desperately. "Isn't it cute?"

"Hey, we better go join everyone—" Allie began.

Dad laughed. "Doesn't everyone call you Kiki?" he asked her.

"Only certain special people," Kiki replied gamely.

Dad laughed. "Thanks! So what do the kids here at camp call you?"

"Oh, it doesn't matter," Kiki said, laughing too gaily. "You know kids! I answer to anything!"

"Miss French! Miss French!" Muffy Sue called, running back over to us. "Could my cousin Lorell please take our picture together?"

With Muffy Sue was Lorell Courtland, one of the two most obnoxious girls on Sunset Island. Lorell and her best friend, Diana De Witt, were both nineteen and they were the mortal enemies of Sam and her friends.

And now Lorell was pointing a camera at Kiki. Muffy Sue put her left arm around Kiki, and threw her right arm up in the air dramatically. "Ready!" she called to Lorell.

Lorell snapped off a shot. "That was just so darling! And, Muffy Sue, honey, you looked precious!" Lorell trilled. "You know, it's so amazin' to me that Sammie never mentioned that the mother of the little girls she babysits for is a famous actress!"

"What are you talking about?" Dad asked, looking totally confused.

"I'm talking about your lovely wife," Lorell said, an evil glint in her eye. "When Muffy Sue came home and told us about Talia French, I just had to come see for myself. It sounded strange to me, I must admit, but then I never judge people," she finished solemnly. She slung the strap of the camera over her shoulder. "Oh, she is your wife the famous actress Talia French, isn't she?" Lorell asked innocently.

Allie and I looked at each other. There was nowhere to run, nowhere to hide. We were going to be the laughingstock of the entire island. And it would be all my fault.

"Oh, silly, Muffy Sue got it all wrong!" Dixie exclaimed.

"I did not," Muffy Sue insisted.

"Yes, sweetie, you did," Dixie corrected her. "See, Muffy Sue just got the parts we're all playing in this play confused with reality!" She bent down and patted Muffy Sue's curls. "It's because you have such a vivid imagination, precious," she added.

"No, I don't—" Muffy Sue began.

"Oh, sure you do," Tori chimed in. "It's this play we're doing, called . . . 'The Actress'! And . . . this lady plays the role of this actress, Talia French!" She turned to Dixie. "Right, Dixie?"

"Right!" Dixie agreed. "And Becky and Allie play the parts of her daughters! I'm so impressed with Muffy Sue," she added to Lorell. "She's so gifted, really!"

Lorell put her hands on her hips. She looked at Muffy Sue. "Muffy Sue . . ." she said warningly.

"But I told you the truth!" Muffy Sue insisted.

"Don't you be too hard on her now," Dixie warned. "A fanciful imagination is just a sign of her great talent!"

"You dragged me all the way over here for nothing!" Lorell snapped at Muffy Sue. "Well, I am just so humiliated!" She turned Muffy Sue around and they hurried off.

I stared at the ground. I could not, but could not, look anyone in the face.

"Girls, would you please tell me what is really going on here?" my father asked in a quiet voice.

I gulped hard, willing myself not to cry. Finally, I looked up at Dixie and Tori. "I guess you figured it out."

"Not really," Tori admitted. "I mean, I guess she's not really your mom, huh?"

I reached for Allie's hand and clutched it tight. "She's an actress," I admitted. "Her name is Kiki Coors. We hired her to pretend to be our mother."

"You *what*!?" my father asked. He rubbed his face. "I don't believe this. . . ."

"I'm sorry, Dan," Kiki said, touching him on the arm.

He turned on her. "How could you do this?"

"We paid her. That's how," I said bluntly.

Kiki bit her lower lip. "Look, I wasn't planning to take your money," she told me. She looked down at the ground and seemed to be trying to get a hold of herself. "I liked pretending to be your mom," she said in a low voice. Then she looked at my father. "About us . . . that's totally real."

My father looked hurt and confused. "I just . . . I don't know why you girls did this," he said.

Neither Allie nor I could answer him.

"They wanted a mother," Kiki finally said gently.

Dad turned away, I guess so we wouldn't see how hard these words were for him to hear. "I'll be back," he mumbled, and walked off. I knew he didn't want us to see him cry.

"I have to go after him," Kiki said, and she hurried to catch up with Dad.

Allie and I were still clutching each other's hands. As for myself, I was hanging on for dear life.

"I guess you hate us now," I muttered to Tori and Dixie. I absolutely refused to let them see me cry.

"Where's your mother, really?" Tori asked.

"We don't know," Allie replied. "She ran away when we were little kids."

"That's terrible!" Dixie cried.

"Don't you dare feel sorry for us," I warned her, holding back my tears.

Dixie was silent a moment. "Okay. I won't feel sorry for you because your mom ran away, if you won't feel sorry for me that my parents treat me like I'm six years old."

"And I won't feel sorry for you if you don't laugh at me for being so stupid around boys," Tori added.

I looked over at Allie.

"I guess we could do that," she agreed cautiously.

I looked at Dixie. "How did you come up with that lie for Muffy Sue so quickly?" I asked her.

"It was kind of brilliant, wasn't it?" she mused. "I don't know! It just popped into my head!"

Tori kicked her sneaker in the dirt. "You know, you could have told us the truth. Even if you wanted to lie to everyone else at camp."

"Yeah?" I asked carefully.

Dixie nodded in agreement. "Y'all, real friends stand by each other. They keep each other's secrets. And that's what we are, real friends!"

"You wanna pinkie on it?" I blurted out.

"Becky!" Allie protested.

"It's okay, Allie," I told her. "It really is."

"What's that?" Tori asked.

"It means we take a solemn vow to stick by each other, no matter what," I explained. Then I raised my hand and stuck my pinkie in the air.

Slowly, Allie's pinkie met mine. "No matter what," she said.

"No matter what," Tori and Dixie echoed. They raised their hands, and our four little pinkies touched.

Bobby blew his whistle and called everyone to come over to the campfire area. In the distance I could see my dad and Kiki, deep in conversation.

"What are you going to do about Kiki and everyone at camp?" Tori asked me.

"I'm going to go ask her to leave," I decided quickly. "She's actually kind of nice, in a weird sort of way. She's nothing like who I thought she was."

"I think she really does like Dad," Allie put in.

"Yeah," I agreed. "We better make sure he knows that. We should ask him to stay, huh?"

Allie nodded and shrugged. "At least we have one parent."

"I don't have the nerve to tell everyone the truth,"

I admitted. "And I think Dad will keep his mouth shut if we ask him to."

"Well, whatever happens, we're with you," Tori said staunchly. A worried look came over her face. "Oh, no, now that Talia French is a fake, I don't have any reason to call Tim with the photo!"

"We'll come up with something. I promise," I assured her.

"Y'all, this is going to be the best summer of our entire lives!" Dixie exclaimed happily.

I looked over at my sister, then at Tori and Dixie, and a big grin spread over my face.

"You ain't just whistling 'Dixie'!" I said, imitating her drawl.

It was going to be a totally amazing summer.

Dear Readers,

Here it is at last—the very first *Club Sunset Island*! I'm so psyched that the book is finally in your hands!

For those of you who are new to the world of Sunset Island—welcome. You have just joined a sisterhood of hundreds of thousands of girls from around the world who share in adventure and romance on one of the greatest islands on earth! You might want to check out the *Sunset Island* books, too!

To all of you faithful *Sunset Island* fans—can you believe the younger teens on the island actually have their own series, too? It was so much fun writing about the island from Becky's point of view. The more I write about her and Allie, the more I like them. And I loved creating Dixie and Tori, too!

You can look forward to many more adventures at Club Sunset Island. The next book, coming this July, is called *Dixie's First Kiss*. All of you Ethan Hewitt fans out there—watch out!

As my longtime readers know, I try to make the *Sunset* books exactly what you want them to be. That's why your letters mean so much to me. Your intelligence, humor, ideas and opinions are what make the island special. I also love getting pictures of you—I put them all up in my office.

I'll pick three letters to be featured in each *Club Sunset Island* book, so when you write, let me know if I can consider your letter for publication, or whether it's private. If your letter is published, I'll send you a free, autographed copy of the book in which your letter appears.

It means so much to me that you care about Sunset Island as much as I do. Thank you for being the coolest, greatest fans any writer could ever hope to have. And remember, I'll keep writing as long as you keep reading!

See you on the island!
Best-
Cherie Bennett

Cherie Bennett
c/o General Licensing Company
24 West 25th Street
New York, New York 10010

CLUB Sunset Island™

Join Dixie, Tori, Becky and Allie for an incredible summer as counselors-in-training at Club Sunset, the new day camp on Sunset Island!

__**TOO MANY BOYS!**   0-425-14252-3/$2.99

A whole boat full of cute boys is beached on Sunset Island–and Becky and Allie have to get ready for Parents' Day.

__**DIXIE'S FIRST KISS**   0-425-14291-4/$2.99

It's the camp's rafting trip and Dixie's finally going to get the chance to spend some time with Ethan Hewitt...if only Patti will leave her alone.   *(Coming in July)*

__**TORI'S CRUSH**   0-425-14337-6/$2.99

Tori's tired of being called a tomboy, but now her athletic abilities may catch the eye of one of the counselors, Pete Tilly.   *(Coming in August)*